Attrition by Simon Lovat

First published 2000 by Millivres Ltd, part of the
Millivres Prowler Group, 3 Broadbent Close, London N6 5GG

World Copyright © 2000 Simon Lovat

Simon Lovat has asserted his right to be identified as the author of this
work in accordance with the Copyright, Designs and Patents Act 1988.

A CIP catalogue record for this book is available from the British Library.

• ISBN 1 902852 12 5

Distributed in Europe by Central Books,
99 Wallis Road, London E9 5LN

Distributed in North America by InBook/LPC Group,
1436 West Randolph, Chicago, IL 60607

Distributed in Australia by Bulldog Books,
PO Box 300, Beaconsfield, NSW 2014

Printed and bound in the EU by WS Bookwell, Finland

ATTRITION
Simon Lovat

Acknowledgements

My thanks are due to my editor, Peter Burton, for steering the novel back to its original form. Many thanks also to Sebastian Beaumont, John McLean and Michael McGachy for their patient reading of various drafts. And special thanks to my father, for the technical equestrian details.

Simon Lovat has worked as an actor for the last fifteen years. He is a prize-winning short story writer, and has been variously published in anthologies and magazines, including *World Wide Writers* and *The Mammoth Book of Gay Short Stories*. He has published one previous novel, *Disorder and Chaos*.

For J and K

attrition *n.* **1 a** the act or process of gradually wearing out, especially by friction. **b** abrasion **2** *Theol.* sorrow for sin, falling short of contrition.

Concise Oxford Dictionary

Throughout the journey northeast, away from London, I had been thinking about my father; persistent, circular thoughts that served only to make me tense. As far as I could remember, he had never so much as hugged me. He certainly never kissed me, of that I was sure. And it wasn't that I was a boy and one didn't show affection to boys, because he was the same with my sister, Hélène. The truth was, Harry was essentially dysfunctional when it came to intimacy; even with his first wife, my mother. I never once saw him kiss her in my entire life. There were probably reasons for this, lying in seclusion in the dark womb of his soul, but in thirty-seven years I had not managed to exhume a single one of them. Now, both my patience and interest had expired and I had given him up as a lost cause.

Callum, my on-again-off-again lover, had been despondent when I'd broken the news to him that I was going. We were lounging on the sofa in my small, dim Kilburn flat at the time, drinking cheap Spanish wine straight from the tetrapack, passing it back and forth like winos.

"What do you mean, you don't know how long you'll be away?" he objected, his soft Scots vowels rising in surprise. "What about me?"

"You'll be fine," I said airily, and waved my arm in a grand gesture of confidence. "There are such things as telephones."

In a perverse way, the situation suited me. Not the fact of going to Bruxley to look after my father without the comforting buffers of other relatives present – that was hideous and terrifying. But I had wanted to cool things off with Callum for some time, and he never seemed to take no for an answer, so a chance to go away somewhere that he couldn't follow seemed a happy solution.

I had already tried, unsuccessfully, to leave Callum on a

number of occasions over the course of our two years together. These partings were often messy, but despite this warning, somehow my resolve would crumble at the last moment and I'd take him back, usually straight to the bedroom. I felt bad about this because a rational corner of my mind knew that Callum wasn't good for me, that our relationship was built on power and obsession rather than love, and every time I took him back another chip of my self-esteem would fall away. Also, I knew that my behaviour made my situation more untenable. Now Callum was fully aware that if he pushed hard enough, he could break me. He understood that when I said 'no', I didn't always mean it. I couldn't see a way out of this emotional quagmire; Callum was too insistent, too good looking to resist. Maybe this break would give me the time and space to decide what I really did want from him.

We had undoubtedly had some good times together, but there were too many areas that caused friction rather than closeness – like the fact that Callum was always borrowing money from me, and never paid it back. The current total was over two hundred pounds. In the light of the fact that I was broke and he was working, this represented a major breakdown of respect.

"Anyway, I thought you hated your father," Callum added, taking a last swig of wine before dropping the empty carton on the floor.

I raised my hand, to silence him. "I've never said that."

Callum's stern face melted into a knowing smile. "And why is it you that's going, and not that sister of yours?" he continued.

I sighed. We'd been through this before. "Because I'm available and she isn't," I replied. "She's a busy lawyer with two children and I'm a terminally unemployed actor. It makes sense."

Callum laughed in a weary, cynical manner. "You need your head examined," he said. "What's wrong with a hospital, or even a nice hospice? They're trained to look after people at those places. What do you know? You can't even put on a Band-Aid, for god's sake."

We both smiled. It was true, I was a poor nurse. Like my father, I hated illness and couldn't bear to be around it. This was a legacy from my mother, Kate; of having watched her wither and die. Even now, some twelve years later, I was still smarting from the wound.

"I agreed to it, and that's that," I told him with a shrug.

Callum let out a low grunt and stared down at his hands. In this attitude of repose his balding, cropped head and sculpted black goatee drew my heart up tight. He looked like a handsome version of Lenin. "You and your weird fucking family," he muttered. Then he looked at me with his large brown eyes and added, "When are you leaving?"

"Tomorrow morning." I looked at my watch. It was late.

"And you've no idea how long you'll be gone?"

I shook my head.

"I wish I could come with you," said Callum as he rose from the sofa in a lithe, catlike movement. "Perhaps when school breaks up?"

"Hmm," I said – the usual non-committal answer. Then I stood up, yawned, and allowed myself to be led to the bedroom.

And now here I was, driving into the heart of Norfolk to stay with Harry, my bellicose parent. It was five years since I had last visited Bruxley, and driving through the village now I felt a curious sensation, a mixture of longing and discomfort. It should have felt like coming home, I'd spent nearly half my life here, or hereabouts, but there was no comforting familiarity – only dread, and the cloying weight of a past I'd hoped I'd left forever. Never had I felt as alien, as external to my surroundings, as I did now, driving to my father's house beneath the vast winter sky. I wanted to lower my head and slip quietly through the village without acknowledging it. The person I had been, the one who had lived here, no longer existed, and my present self didn't belong.

I drove past the old pond, fringed by reeds and home to a small flotilla of ducks. The still depths, currently bereft of water fowl, absorbed the brilliance of the cobalt winter sky, containing it within its small borders before beaming it back up again. Further on, a rough stone cross stood in the centre of the Green as if it had grown up out of the ground, bearing witness to the history of the village, to the simple men who had lost their lives in two world wars.

The Green, pristine and picturesque in a mannered, over-tended way, seemed a reflection of the smug self-satisfaction of the wealthy, empty headed people who lived here now. Their lives were ordered and comfortable, and they wanted a village Green which projected that image of themselves as they drove past in their fast, expensive cars. These were not the farming folk who had worked in the surrounding fields and sent their sons and husbands away to war. These were well-off, horsey people. The kind of people my father had aspired to emulate but, being an ex-jockey rather than a wealthy gentleman, had never quite become. All their houses were set back from the road, down gravel or tarmac driveways, and sat in squat serenity on large plots of land. The winter trees, now stripped of their dense camouflaging summer foliage, allowed them to be revealed in their overblown glory as I passed.

I drove on through the village. Everything about it struck me as horribly familiar, yet too clean and quiet, as if in my absence it had been razed to the ground and then

4

rebuilt – a replica of itself with some small invisible element missing. None of it touched my heart.

Only as I passed the grey-black flint church did I feel any connection with my past, and even then I defied memory to haunt me. That was the end of Kate. That dark, rough hewn, reductionist building housed the hugeness that was my mother. But I would not think about that, I told myself. Instead, I allowed in another memory, a memory of our footsteps ringing in the lane as we walked to that same church beneath a crisp midwinter sky iridescent with the light of hard, tiny stars.

It was Christmas eve, the year I was ten. Hélène and I were bundled up against the cold, struggling to keep awake, cocooned in hats, scarves, overcoats and mittens as we made our way to the church for the midnight service. We slouched along with our sleepy walk, our faces growing chilly in the night air. Kate was up ahead.

Harry, of course, was not with us. He had refused to come on the grounds of atheism, and had forgone the pleasure of driving us to the church, and back again – it was only a mile and a half, he said – because he had a more important date with a bottle of whisky at the Shepherd and Dog. Kate was unable to drive, so we went on foot.

"Why do we have to walk?" Hélène complained, her voice a chain-saw whine. She was fourteen.

"Because it's nicer," said our mother, her voice firm, artificially bright.

"It's not nicer. It's freezing," said Hélène as she wrapped her scarf more tightly about her exposed neck.

"Of course it's nicer. Just look at those stars!"

Kate was passionate about things. What she liked, she loved, and stars were a wonder to her. She could name and identify every constellation in the sky, including those in the Southern hemisphere, and point out prominent individual suns, reeling off their importance, magnitude, and probable distance from the earth. She revelled in notions of time dilation and dark matter, she knew where secret invisible galaxies were hidden, and she marvelled at the sheer scale of the mathematics that defined them. Happiness, for her, was a dark, cloudless night with no moon. She would often spend such nights out in the garden, her bright, wistful face tilted skywards, binoculars slung around her neck, with star charts and a thermos of coffee by her side. The only thing she loved more than stars was painting.

"That's Cygnus, the swan," Kate said. She pointed upward, directly over our heads, at the familiar cruciform constellation.

We stopped in the road and looked up, all three of us. There were no nearby houses to bleed light into our eyes, and the sky was bottomless black. As I looked, stars began to appear out of the blackness, layers and layers of them behind the obvious brighter ones. The ghost ribbon of the Milky Way arched above us. I felt that this sky, more than anything else, was Christmas. Here was something larger than me, beyond my comprehension.

"I can't see a swan," I said.

"No. But that's what it's called."

We walked on again, and Hélène at once returned to the earthly question in hand, unimpressed by the distraction of the heavens. She could never leave something until it was fully answered, especially when it concerned our father. She believed that unanswered questions usually had a lie in them, somewhere.

"Why didn't dad come with us?" she said.

"Because."

"Because?"

"Yes. Because."

"That's not a proper answer," Hélène sighed, and stopped dead in the road. Our mother walked on.

"I'll tell you why. Because he's an atheist," I said to Hélène quietly. It was the only thing I admired about my father.

6

"Anyway, I'm glad he's not here. I hate him."

"I'm telling mum you said that."

"You'd better not."

"And what are you going to do about it, Glory Boy?"

"I'll say you told me what a twat was."

"I didn't!"

"But that's what I'll tell her. You know how she hates that word."

"You'll be sorry if you do. Glory Boy."

"Stop calling me that."

"But that's what you are, though, Glory Boy," Hélène wheedled. "You think you're so good at riding, don't you? Well, you're not."

"I'm better than you!"

At this, Hélène quickly stepped behind me and, unobserved by our mother, pushed me in the back with considerable force. She was bigger and heavier than me, and her strength was such that I careened right into the dark, frosted hedgerow. A short twig poked me in the eye as I fell against the hedge, where I lay for some moments, breathless and suddenly furious. Hélène laughed as I sputtered and cursed, but didn't break her stride.

I let her walk on ahead for a moment, then leapt up and ran after her, mad with rage. When I was within striking distance, I launched myself into a flying rugby tackle and caught Hélène just below the knees with my shoulder, just as I'd been taught at school, and brought her down on the hard road. Hélène let out a startled cry as we both fell to the ground with a heavy, coat-padded thud, and my mother looked round in stunned amazement to see us grappling with one another in the middle of the road, emitting grunts and muttered oaths.

"Stop that!"

Kate's enormous voice cracked the still night open like thunder, and we froze in mid fight. When Hélène and I fought, which we did often, only she could separate us.

7

"One of these days I'm going to kill you," Hélène whispered, her face triumphant in the moonlight.

Hélène had her knee pressed against my stomach; I had a handful of her voluminous hair. We were both consumed by momentary all-encompassing, but ultimately ephemeral, hatred of one another. Our eyes glittered blackly in the night.

"What are you doing, Philip? Just what..." But my mother couldn't finish the sentence. She was too surprised to be properly angry.

"She started it," I complained, still lying in the road. Suddenly I had a mind not to get up. I didn't want to go to the carol service anyway.

"No I didn't. You did."

"Liar."

I pulled Hélène's hair. Hélène let out a little high-pitched scream, for theatrical effect, and in retaliation delivered a swift blow to my face with her free hand. My head, caught off-balance, smacked against the cold road, bumping the ridge of bone beneath my eyebrow. I felt the skin split, and the warmth of running blood. I sat up, touching the wound with my fingers, and began to cry.

"I'm bleeding," I wailed.

Kate, properly angry now, strode towards us and yanked Hélène to her feet with remarkable force.

"Why are you doing this, at your age, Hélène?" Kate's face was flushed, her passion for stars now transmuted into a desire for justice. "If there's one thing I can't stand, it's a bully, and that's just what you are," she said. "You're practically twice his size."

Hélène said nothing, and bent down to examine her jeans, inspecting them for damage. They were her favourite jeans, big bell flares, faded and thin at the knee; the ones she wore to go riding, with the names of her favourite ponies written all across the thighs in red biro. Kate had wanted her to wear something

8

else for the service, something more befitting her age and gender, but Hélène had refused, threatening not to come at all if she couldn't wear them. Looking at them now, I was pleased to see that our tussle had resulted in a tear right through her declaration of love for a horse called Charlie.

"Now behave, both of you," said Kate. "Here," she added, handing me a small hanky to wipe the blood from my eye. "Now come on."

We walked the rest of the way to the church in silence, the space between us getting larger and larger until it filled the whole night. Why did it always have to be like this? I wondered. I didn't understand why Hélène and I were enemies and rivals. I only knew that it was something that had arisen soon after the arrival of Blackberry, our first pony, and I had no idea how to change it.

We'd fought over everything from then on. We both wanted the black melaware cereal bowl at breakfast, and scrapped over that; we both wanted to eat with the Plaza spoon, the one my mother 'accidentally' stole from the hotel on her honeymoon; we both wanted to ride Blackberry at the same time; we always wanted to watch different, conflicting, tv programmes; and we both wanted to be the boot when we played Monopoly. All these things produced disproportionate rage in the two of us, a wordless fury whose only outlet was combat. It was for this reason that we never shared a bedroom. We were kept apart at night.

Hélène always won our fights because she was bigger, stronger, more wily than me. Perhaps, too, she needed to win more badly than I did. In all the years we fought, I never vanquished her. The nearest I got to it was in our famous Ten Pound fight – our highest profile, final fight, staged in the sitting room of our parental home – and even that was something of a Pyrrhic victory, more resembling a truce.

9

Leaving the village, I turned left down the lane from which I'd gazed up at Cygnus, and passed the spot where Hélène had cracked my head on the road. If I was to drive on down this briar-flanked lane I would arrive at my first childhood home, an unobtrusive square brick building close to the village school, and the repository of my earliest memories; the house in which Kate had been well and happy. But that was not my destination.

The year after our Christmas brawl in the road, my father's parents were killed in a road accident, leaving Harry a sum of money which he spent on Ravencrag – a remote, bizarre building with several paddocks and enough stabling for twelve horses. The stables had not been used for years and were run down and in disrepair. This lowered the value, and also rendered Ravencrag an unattractive investment to the casual buyer. Because of this, the yard had proved difficult to sell, and the vendors let Harry beat the price down still further, to an affordable level. We moved there the following summer, in the year I was twelve, with everything we owned crammed into one large removal van because my father wanted to do it in one trip. Hélène and I sat in the back of the van, squashed amongst the furniture, whilst the family dogs leapt about, yelping in excitement.

Our new home was eleven miles from our previous one, four miles from the nearest other building, and, to Kate's dismay, ten miles from the nearest town. The land stretched out from the house in all directions, and was completely encircled by a mature beech wood, End Wood, which made us feel that Ravencrag was an island.

It was Harry's pipe-dream come true. Ever since his blighted days as a jockey, he had yearned to run a yard of his own, and now he had one. Hélène, too, was delighted with it, as were the dogs, but my mother and I were far from pleased to be here, in no man's land, surrounded by horses and hemmed in by trees. The only saving grace was the house itself, which was extraordinary and charming.

My father worked hard on the dilapidated yard and spent a year renovating the stables. We all helped him, with varying degrees of enthusiasm. We carried timbers, painted fences with creosote, and transported saws, hammers and buckets of nails from place to place as Harry needed them. Kate and I took part in a lacklustre fashion, knowing that we were not building our dreams, but Harry's. For us, there would be no reward at the end of all the work. When the yard was ready, Harry signed up his old friend Arthur, another ex-jockey, to be his business partner, and together they opened up as a thoroughbred rehabilitation centre. They made gradual improvements as they went along, including a long, gently curving gallop on the inside edge of End Wood, complete with two practice fences. Ostensibly, this was for their personal amusement – Harry hoped to train his own horses here – but it was an impressive facility and helped to attract clients.

As I wound my way down these still, familiar lanes, I swallowed, and tried to quiet the rising clamour of my thoughts. Here, on the right, was the beginning of my father's land, screened by those mature beeches – rustling green in summer, now brittle charcoal-drawn silhouettes against the giant East Anglian sky. I wondered if they had grown since I was last here. Did trees keep on growing for ever? To me, they looked the same as always, only dead. It suited my mood perfectly.

I still couldn't believe that I was actually doing this, that I was driving to Ravencrag in order to take up residence with my father. It was no longer an abstract notion, but real; a hard, cold fact which lay in my stomach like a lump of frozen steel. None of us had expected it to happen so soon, and I hadn't had time to adjust my thoughts to the reality of it. Barely four months had passed since Hélène and I had first discussed it, as we lounged together in her garden, back in the summer.

I had known that something was wrong as soon as I arrived at her Chorleywood home and found her alone. I was under the impression that a family barbecue had been planned. We usually had a couple of these every summer – one in my tiny, soot-blackened back yard in Kilburn, and one in her croquet-lawn sized garden. I had been looking forward to it. Ewan, a quiet scientist who wore a collar and tie at all times, provided a perfect counterpoint to our loud personalities, and the children were always a pleasure to be around.

"Where's Ewan and the kids?" I asked as my sister ushered me into the house.

"Oh, Bryony insisted that they had to go and see the new Spielberg film, and today's their last chance," said Hélène. She was trying to sound casual, but I sensed a certain tension in her tone.

I looked up at my big sister. Since our fractious childhood, we had discovered, as adults, that we liked one another, united in our resentment of our father. Four years older than me, she had, by some random chance, monopolized the family's large genes, and towered above the rest of us like some mythical goddess. She was blonde, big boned and beautiful, with the body of a swimmer; my father and I were elfin, diminutive and dark, like nervous Jews. Hélène was a good five inches taller than me in her stockinged feet, and she was currently augmenting this with a pair of serious heels. I felt like a midget as I stared up at her, and was at once reminded of my agent, who persisted in telling me that I didn't work because I was short. He'd been telling me this, in our twice-weekly phone conversations, for five years, as if I could somehow become six foot by force of will. I was not happy with my agent, but then I didn't know any actor who was.

"So what's new?" I said, and smiled.

My sister smiled back, but it didn't ignite and looked false. She led me into the garden, where we sat in two up-market green and white striped lawn chairs. Between us was a small wooden table on which stood a refreshing looking pitcher of Pimms and two glasses. She poured us both a drink, then removed the light t-shirt she was wearing to reveal a smart swimsuit, slipped on a pair of Ray-Bans, and sat back in her chair. For some moments neither of us spoke – an unusual occurrence.

I pulled off my own shirt and let it fall in a heap by my side. "Hey, it's the Bay Watch babe," I called, in an attempt to shake off the increasing feeling of dread which had crawled over me like a shadow. I wished Ewan and the children were there.

"Hardly. I'm twenty-five years too old," she replied.

"But you do look glamorous," I said.

It was true. Her skin had taken a wonderful honey coloured tan, offsetting the blondness of her hair, which had lightened in the sun. The fashionable shades completed the not-quite-famous film star look.

"I don't," she laughed.

"Okay, you don't."

I looked at her and shook my head in wonder. Hélène took no exercise, except to ride horses – which she had little time for, now that her career had taken off – and yet she possessed this amazing, and enviable, physique. I, on the other hand, had to sweat in gyms, and jog for miles to maintain my fitness. There was no god.

"Here," she said, proffering the pitcher of Pimms for a refill.

I stood up and refreshed my glass, then flopped down again, drained by even this simple activity in the face of the acetylene glare of the unrelenting sun.

"You're looking good yourself," she said as I settled back into my chair.

I shrugged. I had the standard physique of an ageing actor.

"I'm losing my hair," I said.

"I thought gay men didn't mind losing their hair?"

"This one does."

"Don't they all cut it really short, like in the army?"

"Yes," I said, "but *I* can't, because it's not versatile enough for casting. If I did that, all I'd get to play would be soldiers, concentration camp victims, and people with Aids."

As the words left my mouth, Hélène's face froze half way between two expressions. She seemed to hesitate, unsure whether to sit or stand. I was reminded of those old B films where a multiple personality wrestles with two warring identities, each vying for supremacy.

"Oh," she said, clearly thrown. She leant down to her handbag, fished out a scrunched up cigarette, lit it, and pulled on it with a succession of short shallow puffs. Calmed, she looked at me with a level expression. "Listen, Pip, there *is* a reason why the others aren't here," she began. "I sent them away." She paused, and looked out over the garden for a moment. "Oh god, there's no easy way to say this, so I'll just say it," she added. "Dad's had the results of his tests."

Harry had complained all spring of a blocked nose. It had started out like a regular cold, but did not develop into anything, and at first nobody took any notice of it. The

14

doctor said it might be an allergy. Meanwhile, Harry's breathing became more and more difficult, until, eventually, he could no longer breathe through his nose at all, and had to pant like a dog, which made eating noisy, and hard work. It was at this stage that the doctor suggested there might be a blockage. This rang alarm bells in all of us. Blockages meant tumours, which meant cancer. Cancer had stolen Kate from us, and its icy hand still squeezed our hearts. It was the family fear. But the doctor insisted that a malignancy was hugely unlikely. A benign growth of some kind was far more probable. This did little to allay our fears, however. They had said the same about Kate.

"As you know, when they operated, they found that the blockage *was* a growth, which they removed. It was the size of a small egg, apparently. And that seemed to be that. Or so I thought. He certainly didn't mention anything else to me. I don't know if he called you?"

Hélène looked at me, and I shook my head. In the history of our relationship, my father had never phoned me.

"But, unfortunately, it wasn't quite as simple as that," said Hélène, and waved a pall of blue cigarette smoke away from her face. She let out another sigh. "I don't know why he waited three weeks to tell us, but he phoned this morning to say that he had bad news. It seems the growth wasn't malignant, but it *was* a kind of cancer."

"Can they treat it?" I cut in.

"Yes and no," said Hélène. "That is, they can treat the site of the tumor, and it won't kill him... But there'll be more."

"What kind of cancer is it?"

"Kaposi's Sarcoma."

I was dumbfounded, my thoughts arrested as abruptly

15

as if I had been struck on the head with a brick. "Are you sure?"

"Yes. That's what he said," my sister told me. "Why are you looking at me like that?"

I took a breath. "First of all, it's unusual for KS lesions to grow big like that," I explained. It was a sad fact that, unwillingly, I had become knowledgeable on this subject over the years. "Kaposi's Sarcoma usually produces small lesions on the skin. And it only affects elderly Jewish or Italian men, or people with compromised immune systems." Héléne's eyes widened with the shock of a slowly dawning realisation. "The cancer itself is moderately benign," I added with a shrug, and looked across at my sister, who was staring at me with her mouth open.

"So he has *Aids?*" she croaked.

"Unless it's not really KS."

"Why would he say it was, if it wasn't?"

"I don't know, 'Lène." I paused and let the afternoon wash over me for a moment. "But how?" I mused aloud. "How on earth has *he* got it?"

Hélène bit her lower lip. "Perhaps he got it from Kate. She had lots of transfusions, didn't she, during her operations? And that was before they started screening blood. Maybe she was HIV positive, and..."

I sat there, feeling quiet inside. I just couldn't picture my father as a person with Aids. "I can't believe it," I said.

"Neither can I," said Hélène in a slow voice. But she was calm.

For my own part, I was shocked by the strangeness of the news, but beyond that I felt nothing. What was wrong with us? We had just discovered that our father was dying, and neither of us was reacting in the manner expected of such news. This, above all, made me feel eerie.

16

"How's he taking it?" I said.

"That's the weird part. You know how he's always hated illness? How he used to go ballistic if any of us ever got so much as a cold? He's taken this like a lamb." Hélène stubbed her cigarette out on the grass and left it there.

"It's the shock," I said. "It'll hit him later."

Hélène shook her head. "I don't think so," she replied. "I think it's because he's found God." And now her voice had begun to wobble, a foreshadowing of tears.

"What?" I cried.

I stared at Hélène in wonder. How could our reactionary, atheist father have found salvation? This news was far more shocking to me than his diagnosis with Aids. It was an infinitely more profound challenge to my model of the world, as I understood it, than his illness.

"That's the worst part!" said Hélène. She was crying now, low, gentle sobs pumping out between her words. "If you could have heard him... He was like a child, or a robot or something. His voice had no expression at all. None. And he kept on saying how *happy* he was, how this was the best thing that had ever happened to him. All in this flat, dead voice. Every sentence was rounded off with 'praise'. It seemed so creepy. I couldn't stand it."

I took her in my arms and she cried loudly against my shoulder as the remorseless sun beamed down from the aching sky. I soothed her, rubbing my right hand in small circles between her shoulder blades, and slowly her tears subsided. Comforted at last, she pulled away and wiped her eyes with the back of her hand.

"Sorry."

"Don't be silly," I said.

We fell silent and I tried, and failed, to imagine my father as a Believer.

"But how did he get converted?" I said at last.

"I don't know. He didn't say. Except that he had some sort of fit, and when he came to, he was saved."

We fell back into our own thoughts. The outside world seemed not to reach us, as if we were cocooned inside a giant soap bubble. We could see out, and others could see in, but we couldn't connect.

"The thing is," said Hélène, returning to her more practical self, "what are we going to do about it?"

"About his conversion?"

"No. His illness."

"Why do we have to do anything about it? What *can* we do?"

"Nothing immediately, of course," said Hélène. "That's not what I mean. The point is, what's going to happen when he gets seriously ill, which he will eventually? What's going to happen then?"

"He'll go into hospital, or a hospice."

Hélène shook her head with vigour, her hair cascading around her shoulders like priceless candy floss. "That won't happen, Pip. You know it won't. Harry is petrified of hospitals of all kinds, after what happened to Kate. He'd never go into one willingly."

"He did for the nose operation," I pointed out.

"But only for a day. He discharged himself as soon as he could."

"If he was very ill, he'd have no choice. We could put him in a hospital, and that would be that."

Hélène looked at me for a moment, a level stare that seemed to dive right into my heart. "You're right, we could do that if we wanted to. But knowing how much Harry hates hospitals, would we be prepared to?"

Fear of hospitals was one thing, at least, that I shared with my father. To me, those slick, quiet corridors smelt of helplessness and death. But his was not an idle dislike – he had a full-blown irrational terror of hospitals, now fed to obesity by Kate's experience. I knew that I could never consign Harry to one and sleep.

"What's the alternative?" I said. "Couldn't we hire a nurse to look after him at home?"

"Maybe. But it's the same argument as hospitals, really. He distrusts nurses as much as he distrusts surgeons, since mum. As far as he's concerned, they're all ignorant seventeen year olds just waiting to marry a handsome doctor. To his mind, it was a nurse who finally killed Kate. I doubt he'd allow himself to be looked after by one."

We stared at one another, the obvious conclusion dawning on us.

"So who's going to do it?" said Hélène.

Sudden birdsong, the insistent bubbling of a hidden blackbird, penetrated our isolated bubble like a needle, releasing us back into the real world. The sun pressed down on my head like a physical weight as I guessed how the play would finish. Despite the summer heat, I felt cold.

I looked at my sister and gave a thin smile. "I don't think it's a good idea. I'm a lousy nurse. I don't even like him. He hates me," I said.

"No he doesn't."

"He does, 'Lène. He really does."

There was a brief, tense pause.

"I have to remain available," Hélène said with a shrug. "I might be in the middle of an important case. I wouldn't be able to drop it with no notice. And of course there are the kids to consider."

So that left me. The child that Harry disliked most. But I nodded in reluctant agreement. "It makes sense, I suppose, from a logical point of view. And besides, you did it last time." I was thinking of Kate, and how my sister had nursed her during those last weeks.

I looked over to the flower bed which ran the length of the garden and was dominated by a large star azalea. It was coming to the end of its season yet still offered a profusion of giant red blooms. Small insects crawled over the petals, absorbed with their insect business, as we let the afternoon wash over us.

"Will you do it, then? When the time comes?" Hélène asked me after a while.

I grunted, eyes half shut against the westering sun. "I don't see any other option," I said.

"That's very stoical of you."

"Is it? Perhaps it's because I can't believe it's ever really going to happen."

"But it will." Hélène sighed and leant over to me, lightly touching my forearm with her hand. "It will."

"What if we fight?" I said. I couldn't remember the last conversation I'd had with my father which didn't end in a row. "It might be hard to resist."

"Don't pre-judge, Pip. You might be surprised. People do change," Hélène said. "Look at us. We used to fight like mortal enemies, didn't we? And now we're friends."

"Yes," I said. "How did that happen?"

"I don't know."

"And why did we fight in the first place?"

"I don't know that, either."

I looked up at the screen of poplars at the end of the garden. "Do you remember that hideous fight we had in the sitting room that time?" I said.

"Which one?" said Hélène evasively.

I turned back to her, surprised. It was not possible that she didn't know which fight I was referring to. It had been the showpiece of our Adolescents From Hell routine.

"The Ten Pound Fight," I reminded her. "On New Year's Eve."

"Oh, that," she said, dismissing it as a trifle. "I barely remember it." And she looked away.

Later, as I drove back home, along the hot, clogged M25, all I could think about was my father.

He was a 'born again' Christian.

He had Aids.

I had agreed to look after him when the time came.

But however much I repeated this cheerless litany to myself, it never once sounded real.

Now, as I neared the house, it struck me that there was a curious rightness about the fact that I would be looking after Harry. There was an appealing symmetry to the reversal of the parent-child roles. A part of this lay in the enormous power I now had at my disposal. I could play God. I could be a benevolent, listening, solicitous nurse – or I could be a demon, repaying him in kind for all the slights, cruelties and shortcomings that his unbending, impervious personality had wrought on our family throughout my childhood. Of course, I knew I wouldn't do that, but nevertheless the fantasy had a rosy aspect.

"Here comes Nurse Annie Wilkes," I said aloud, but the irony was bitter to my ear.

End Wood now gave way to a curving driveway on the right, down which my father's house stood. I turned down it, and drove past a large wooden hoarding set on the grass verge, emblazoned in careful gold lettering against a background blue as a robin's egg, which announced that it was one mile to Ravencrag Yard. It looked exactly like the signs which stand at the gates of public schools – lavish, self-important signs inviting wealthy people to spend large sums on an absurd, debatable luxury. No doubt my father had done this deliberately. His was not a racing yard, it was a kind of retirement home for racehorses which had broken down, or needed resting for other reasons – an equine equivalent of a Swiss mountain cure – and people needed persuasion to entrust their stock into his care. A sign such as this suggested class, a superior brand of care available only to the elite, and it seemed that the tactic worked. People were more than willing to part with large sums in order to have Harry nurse their horses back to health, rather than turn them out to grass for a year, on their own land, to achieve the same result. I had never understood this, until Harry explained: Many owners didn't have any land of their own, and his yard fees were a good deal cheaper than the racing yards, where the injured horse would be simply confined to a loose box and ignored until it recovered – if it did at all. Consequently, his business thrived.

Paddocks lay on either side of the driveway now, dotted with thoroughbreds wrapped in New Zealand rugs. Those nearest the road watched me pass with passive eyes, then ambled off on their impossible stick legs. I watched them go and wondered at their power to transfix Hélène and Harry. Those two could lean on a gate and stare at the horses for hours, drinking up their ungainly grace, their scent, their swiftness and stupidity, but they held no fascination for me.

As a child I had ridden horses and enjoyed it, but not out of a visceral admiration of their animal power. I had enjoyed it for the pleasure of mastering a difficult skill, of learning all the tricks. I was interested only in the showmanship of riding. Racing itself, the end to which both Hélène and myself were being groomed, had seemed massively dull and I much preferred show jumping, of which Harry disapproved. It was Hélène who harboured all the enthusiasm, who worked for hours in the stables for no money, and turned the horses out when Harry and Arthur were busy. I went near the horses as little as possible. To me they were like machines, the maintenance of which was tedious and exacting, whereas Hélène loved everything about them, happily mucking out, grooming, feeding and watering them in all her spare time. Curiously, this did not please Harry. It served only to exacerbate his frustration that it was not me, the boy-child, who was showing an interest, and both Hélène and I suffered for that. A further ugly twist of fate, which rubbed salt into the wound of my indifference, was that I was gifted with natural flair, and often did well in the hunter trials which my father insisted we both took part in. I'd regularly beat Hélène, and amassed an impressive array of cups – but I never wanted to be a jockey.

I rounded the last curve of the quiet drive and the house came into view, bright in the watery January sunshine. I looked up at its gothic grey frontage and smiled. I loved this house; there was no other like it. Two centuries before, the builder had erected this single monument to his family and then ran out of money, ruined. As testament to this history, his weathered family coat of arms was affixed to the wall where one of the upstairs windows should have been. Behind it was the bedroom that had been mine.

I hadn't always liked Ravencrag. It had caused us much embarrassment as children, when inviting friends to stay. They had invariably stared up at it, open mouthed, for a full minute before declaring that we lived in a castle. It wasn't until I grew older that I began to appreciate the eccentricities of this cold, rambling folly of a house, with its thirty foot archway that straddled the drive, its bone-white turrets, its fussy crenellations and narrow, recessed windows. It was years before I forgave Ravencrag its pretensions to grandeur. Now, my private fantasy was to reduce the building to its component parts, brick by brick, and reassemble it in London like a miniature Tower.

In truth, the house was smaller than it looked from the outside, like Doctor Who's tardis in reverse. The body of the building comprised of four large rooms, two up, two down, and a square box-turret which housed a dark spiral stairway. The rest of the house sprawled behind a low crenellated facing wall, and consisted of a small coat room, a hallway, a kitchen, two bathrooms, and a long narrow corridor which led, eventually, to a spacious L-shaped sitting room. Although there were plenty of windows, they seemed to let in little light and the house always remained damp and dark. I often felt that I was living underground.

It was a strange place, without doubt. The damp affected my mother, who had a weak chest; I claimed that my room was haunted; and Hélène, the giant of our diminutive family, had problems with the low doorways. And there were other quirks to the house, further secrets which we discovered gradually over the years: Certain doors would open only if pressure was applied to exactly the right spot; certain treads of the stair would groan at particular hours of the night; clocks never kept good time; the cats would never go into the stairwell; when Kate sang a particular note, in the dining room, the windows resonated in answer. And the summer I was fifteen, I found a swarm of butterflies in the walk-in larder, a mist of pale blue chalky wings fluttering about my astonished head like confetti. The house was forever surprising us in this way, delivering up new mysteries like incomprehensible gifts.

I slowed down, sliding past the kitchen window which looked directly on to the drive, and rolled on through the archway. As I parked in the small courtyard to the rear of the house, which backed on to the garden, I knew that I was far from prepared to see my father, that I was not reconciled to it at all. Still gripping the steering wheel with tension-whitened knuckles, I stared through the filthy

24

windscreen, my eyes vacant, and took several deep breaths, breathing from the diaphragm as I'd been taught at drama school all those years ago. My heart was banging in my chest so hard that it was almost audible. I was more nervous than I'd ever been and I could feel the bitter sting of bile rising in my throat.

I left my bags in the car and let myself into the garden via the wooden latch gate. I felt light-headed, my legs wobbly as those of a new-born lamb. As I made my way, slowly, to the front door, I looked up at the vast yew tree which had always dominated the garden – holding court over its acolytes of lilac and cherry trees, which my sister and I had grown from pips – and felt its glowering darkness enter me. This was going to be harder than I had expected.

As I knocked on the door I tried to establish what I felt about being here again, my favourite eleventh hour tactic, but nothing came up. That was the problem I had with Harry, there was nothing specific I could hang my disgruntled hat on. I had no clean feelings about him. I had not been allowed the luxury of simple dislike, a neat and clearly defined emotion. My feelings had always carried the ungainly bulk of compromise, shifting from disdain to resentment and ambivalence – and back again – as constantly as the tides, throughout the years of my childhood and adolescence. Now, of course, I recognised that I also felt something else: a grudging pity. After all, Harry had Aids. If nothing else, I could respond to that. I kept reminding myself of that, over and over in my head, as I waited for him to come to the door. It was a feeble litany which did little to calm my mounting anxiety, born of the fact that we had not spent any time together for years, and certainly not alone. I couldn't imagine how it was going to be.

Eventually, the door opened to reveal Harry with a rictus of a smile hanging on his thin face.

"Praise!" he said in a faint throaty voice. "You're here."

I winced inside, embarrassed by his born-again smile and greeting. I always thought of Harry as a godless reactionary, and it threw me off-kilter to be reminded of his recent conversion. It seemed to have eliminated his personality, ripping it from his body in a cleansing wave of righteous fervour but leaving nothing in its place. I'd spent my life building a wall against his rage and indifference, but it crumbled in the face of this anodyne, smiling, non-person. I felt naked and defenceless against him in this zombie state. I tried to smile back.

"Come on in," my father said, gesturing with a small arm.

He was swathed in sweaters, which padded his tiny body, and wore brown slippers. A pair of round wire-rimmed reading glasses perched on his nose, lending him a false air of intelligence.

I hesitated on the threshold, the smile falling from my face. It was five years since I'd set foot in his house. Five years since I'd stormed off with Rob, my lover at the time, in a welter of self-righteous indignation, vowing never to return again.

"How dare you treat us like this?" I'd shouted, appalled at Harry's insistence that Rob and I should sleep in separate rooms. "I'm thirty one years old and I will not be treated like a child!"

We had stayed less than an hour.

Suddenly I was angry with my sister for putting me through this. Of the two of us, surely I was by far Harry's more unwelcome nurse? It was ridiculous that I should be here, that I should be asked to shelve my past resentments, now grown to the size of a mountain, and walk into Harry's house. I glanced up at the gritty grey door lintel, reluctant to step beneath it. As soon as I walked into the house, everything past would be suspended, forgotten, and there was much that I wanted to remember. I looked at Harry, and it seemed that he, too, was reliving that vitriolic moment which had been so crucial to our estrangement.

"Come on, Fy, if you're coming," he said, impatient. "You're letting the cold in."

I took a breath and stepped into the coat room, pulling the heavy door shut behind me. As it closed, I felt the past swim up to claim me. Although it was five years since I'd been here last, I had only visited a handful of times in the preceding seven, and everything reminded me of Kate, catapulting me back twelve years. All that was missing were the dogs, who always ran up to greet visitors, whose animal noises filled the house at all times as they wandered from room to room searching for a suitable spot to curl up and sleep. It was their absence, as much as the absence of my mother, that made the house feel like a mausoleum. Dark, cold, bereft. I looked about me and tears pricked my eyes, but did not fall.

Harry moved to my side. "It's okay," he said, laying his birdlike hand on my arm, his tone softening. "It's going to be fine."

I was embarrassed, and amused, that Harry had presumed my tears were for him. I was also confused by his concern, and the lightness of his solicitous hand on my arm. That he had touched me at all was astonishing – I couldn't recall the last time we'd had physical contact of any kind. On the rare occasions that we met, we never even shook hands.

Harry lifted his hand from my arm and walked into the hall, and down the corridor. "Come into the drawing room,

Fy," he said over his shoulder. "It's the only place I can keep warm."

In the sitting room we sat in large padded armchairs by the black Norwegian stove, the one I'd stared into for hours on the night I heard that Kate was dying, and a melancholy silence threatened to engulf me. I forced myself to speak. I felt that if I didn't say something now, this minute, I would remain mute forever.

"So how are you?" I said.

It was scarcely an original line, and fatuous under the circumstances, but it broke the silence. As I said it, I found myself checking his face, permanently set into an arrogant, thin-lipped sneer, for KS lesions, and was relieved to find none. I had not looked before, afraid that I might recoil in a reflex action of surprise and shock if I was to locate one nestling on a cheek, in his thin white hair, or perhaps on the back of his hand. So long as he looked outwardly normal, healthy, I would be able to manage; I would be able to ignore the fact that, even now, lesions were swelling in secret, forming hard purple-brown lumps inside him, and on parts of his body that I could not see. But it was of paramount importance to me that his face remained clear. A terrible attitude for a nurse, I knew. But then I wasn't a nurse.

"I'm not so bad," Harry replied, his eyes shining with feverish light, "I'm just tired. I sleep a lot." He coughed, a weak ineffective convulsion. "But now there's something up with my bone marrow. It's made me a bit feeble."

I already knew this. That was why I was here – to help Harry up and down the stairs, to fetch and administer medicines, to watch him slowly fade. I wondered if Harry was aware of his prognosis. The doctor had told me that he would die within a month, maybe two.

"But you feel all right?" I said.

28

Harry nodded, a tiny movement of his craggy, grey-haired head. "I feel fine," he said.

"What about the horses?"

"Arthur is looking after all that," Harry explained with a wave of his hand. It was a cross between a half-bored regal salute to the people, and a lacklustre attempt to swat a fly. "I've not been up to it for months."

I nodded, already having run out of conversation, and another silence wrapped itself around us like a tourniquet. The air seemed clogged with past recrimination, which insincere platitudes could not penetrate. I shifted in my seat as the garish Swiss cuckoo clock above me, painted bright green and red, ticked its loud, insistent life-seconds one by one into the dead room. Hélène had brought it back from a school skiing trip some twenty-five years before, and it had hung on that wall, in that exact same spot, ever since. I glanced at my father, who was looking at his feet, then I stared into the stove again, at the scintillating orange embers of the fire, and wondered how much of this silence I would be able to endure.

"Arthur will be pleased to see you," Harry said at last.

"I'll go and say hello, later," I replied.

There was another tight pause.

"Arthur loves having Delaware Gold here," Harry added, smiling, after a moment. "Odds on he'll mention him as soon as he sees you."

That sounded familiar. "Should I know that name?" I said.

Harry puffed out his sunken cheeks in surprise, and looked at me over the top of his reading glasses.

"I should say so!" he said. "Delaware Gold is class, and no mistake. But he's been out of racing for a while. He won the Gold Cup two years ago but broke down rather badly afterwards. Then he had tendon trouble in his nearside

29

foreleg. He's trained by Smallwood, you know, who Arthur used to ride for, so they sent him to us. We tried resting him, but he didn't turn the corner, so we had to fire him."

I winced. Firing, I recalled, was a brutal form of treatment for severe tendon problems, which involved searing a horse's leg with red hot irons in order to stimulate blood flow and promote healing. I'd seen it done a few times as a child, and found it upsetting. It was extremely painful for the horse. But it did work.

"Del's been with us for ten months now, and he's recovering nicely," my father went on. "And what a little horse he is, Fy! A perfect gentleman. The most genuine ride I ever had. Four year old, with the sweetest mouth... Needs good, kind hands." Harry nodded down at my lap. "Perfect for you," he added.

And all at once I knew how we would fill these barren hours over the coming weeks: Harry would speak to me about horses. The realisation came as something of a relief, as I had been fretting, unsure of how we could possibly negotiate them. Harry, sensing this, had taken the initiative, resorting to a subject on which he was an expert, where he would always know more than me. It was his way of asserting his superiority, and his message was clear: He was the parent and I was the child.

Suddenly I sneezed, feeling a tickle in my nose from the dog hair which still clung to the carpets, and some of the furniture, even now. It was four years since Oberon, the last of the pointers, had died, but those needling white hairs were tenacious, and had woven themselves into the fabric of the house. We might move on, I thought, and relinquish Ravencrag to other hands, but unless they were to rip out every carpet, every fixture and fitting, and scrub the building from top to bottom, the dog hair would remain.

"Excuse me," I said, wiping my nose with a hanky.

"You haven't got a cold, have you?" Harry asked warily.

"No," I said. "It's the dog hair."

Harry harumphed, unconvinced, and seemed to shrink into his chair. It was oddly fascinating to see my father reduced in this way, distilled to a fearful husk of himself by disease. He had always enjoyed an iron constitution, and believed that illness of any kind was the product of a weak will. Now he knew differently. Now he was afraid of a common cold.

Later, I told him the way things were going to be:

"You need to rest," I said, "so I'm going to do all the cooking from now on." I watched as he accepted the news with something like resignation. "How have you been managing until now?"

Harry shrugged in his baggy sweaters. "Arthur brings me things sometimes. Otherwise it's just bread, cheese, biscuits," he said. "But I don't eat much," he went on. "It's the drugs they're giving me. They've nipped my appetite."

Harry gestured to his leather-topped writing desk – which stood against the far wall and was covered with a bewildering array of packets, bottles, and tubes of varying shapes and sizes – with the pride of a child showing off his collection of toy soldiers.

"There's more upstairs," he told me cheerfully.

"How are you getting on with them all?"

"All right. But they make me dizzy. Sick, too. That's why I don't eat."

When the time came for me to cook, I saw what he meant. As I inspected the larder, the fridge, and every cupboard in the kitchen, I discovered that there was next to nothing in the house. Evidently, Harry had stopped shopping. In the old days the larder had been kept full, and every cupboard shelf had been crammed with bulk-bought

31

produce – customary when one lives in an isolated house ten miles from the nearest town. But not now. There was nothing in the freezer either, except a grey, dodgy-looking chicken and some pears which I'd remembered seeing on a previous visit, which dated them at something more than five years old.

With mounting exasperation, increased by my own hunger, I went back into the sitting room, where Harry was reading the latest Dick Francis. He was sitting enveloped in his chair, angling the pages so they caught the syrupy yellow light of the table lamp at his shoulder, his glasses pulled down to the end of his nose to exaggerate the prescription.

"There's no food in the house," I exclaimed. "Nothing at all."

Harry looked up from his book. "Isn't there? I'm sure there's bread, and biscuits. And cheese, too. Arthur gave it me only yesterday."

"That's not food – not proper food," I said, suddenly appalled by the weight, the sheer size, of the task I'd shouldered in taking on my stoic, bull-headed, born-again father. "You've got to eat properly, dad. You've got to look after yourself. Have proper meals."

Harry gave me a chilling, uncomprehending stare over the top of his glasses, as if the idea of food, or looking after himself, were alien concepts dreamt up by the Nazis.

"I'll go into town and get some things," I said. "Is there anything special you want?"

Harry thought for a moment, then shook his head and returned to his book.

I drove back into Bruxley, winding through those dark lanes, hoping to find a shop still open at this hour, but convenience stores had yet to penetrate deepest rural Norfolk. I drove on to Fakenham. There I found a small supermarket, with its friendly light spilling out into the surrounding darkness like an oasis, and I stocked up on all the basic foodstuffs. I was their only customer. Several of the staff were taking advantage of this and loitered in the aisles, chattering to one another about the vagaries of inconstant boyfriends in their delightful, rural accents. I paid with plastic and, as the woman behind the counter swiped my card through the machine, I began to worry about money. I didn't have any. It had cost me a large chunk of my giro cheque to pay for the petrol to get here. I certainly couldn't afford grocery bills as well. Swallowing a bitter pellet of anxiety, I determined to ask Harry for a reimbursement later, but this made me feel guilty.

As I drove back to Ravencrag I realised that I was drained, partly through stress and partly through bona fide fatigue. It was only seven thirty but I was already looking forward to going to bed. This was something I hadn't anticipated and it made me feel old.

On my return, I prepared a meal of fish fingers, beans, and mashed potatoes, hardly the height of nutrition or culinary experience but better than the meal Harry would have made for himself. We ate in the under-water-blue dining room, which always reminded me of an aquarium in which we were the fish, and the rest of the house was the outside world. It was Harry's idea to eat here. He couldn't bear to eat off a tray on his lap, so we sat opposite one another across the highly polished dining table, enduring the cold and eating in silence. Our cutlery clattered loudly on our plates, measuring out time in squeaks and scrapes. A light wind sighed against the large picture windows which looked out over the garden, and the dry vine stems of the honeysuckle which climbed around them tapped against the glass like the fingers of the dead.

Harry picked at his child-sized portion of food with all the enthusiasm of an anorexic schoolgirl. I watched him cutting his fish fingers into small pieces – he'd insisted on having only two – and chasing them around his plate, looking busy but eating little. He'd taken a small mouthful of beans five minutes beforehand, which he appeared still to be chewing.

"Not hungry?" I said.

Harry shrugged.

"At least have some potato."

Harry dropped his cutlery on to his plate with the aplomb of a gun-slinger, and looked at me. "Don't nag me, Fy," he said. His tone was hard, granite.

"You've got to eat," I persisted.

"Eat this?" said Harry. He jabbed at a piece of fish finger with the tines of his fork, then held it up for me to see. "This junk food? It must have taken you all of five minutes to whip up this little masterpiece. Why should you care if I eat it or not?"

I said nothing, and thought, *Anger's okay. Anger's normal.* My own stomach balled into a steel fist, extinguishing my appetite with a twist of its powerful fingers.

"I'm trying to help," I said through clenched teeth.

"You might as well leave now, if all you're going to do is nag."

I looked at my father across the table. His eyes were alive, alight. They were the eyes of the old Harry, the Harry underneath the new-born, brainwashed replica I'd been presented with earlier in the day. I preferred him like this. I knew what to expect. I'd rather fight with a bear than dance with a dish-rag. But as if he'd heard my thoughts, the light in Harry's eyes went out, and he lowered his head and stared down at his plate.

"Jesus forgive me," he murmured, apparently

34

addressing his food, then looked up at me with moist eyes. "I'm sorry, Fy, I didn't mean that. It's a lovely meal. Thank you for making it." His voice had returned to its lobotomized calm.

I was confused beyond measure, bereft of all anchors. The shock of this attack, coming out of nowhere, had taken me by surprise, but the instant about face, limp with platitudes, left me with even more to think about. It seemed that Harry was a human volcano, and the magma of his real self was capable of erupting through the fissures in the thin veneer of his new religion at any time. I assumed that I had caused it. My physical presence at the table had reminded him of his past – his past self. Growing up in that house, eating had been a ritual of abuse, rancour and venom. Few meals were ever completed with the full complement of family still seated at the table. Perhaps Harry's outburst was no more than a knee-jerk reaction, a ghost of the countless rows we'd had over meals in the past?

"Okay," I said.

The word arrived between us as a non-committal grunt. Even I wasn't sure what it meant. As it died in the air, a thick silence closed round it and swam about our heads for a full five minutes. Only the wind, and my own gulping and chewing, filled my ears.

Eventually, Harry offered an olive branch of conversation.

"So what's this job of yours that I've been hearing about?" he said as he speared a single baked bean with his fork. "In the West End."

I sighed. Bad news, like news of a death, has to be repeated over and over again, and grinds the teller into smaller and smaller pieces with each repetition, until he turns to dust. And just when he is sure he has told everyone, someone else always appears who doesn't know, and the story must be trotted out once again, dragging his heart behind it, bumping down the road of disappointment and gathering bruises all the way.

"What have you heard?" I said.

"Hélène told me that you've been offered a part in *Wuthering Heights*," my father said. "In London."

"*Top Withins*, the musical," I told him.

"Oh? And when does it go on?"

"That's the tricky part. It doesn't."

"You got the job and now there's no show?"

I nodded. "That's right. The chap playing the main part, Mitch Waugh, got cold feet and pulled out."

"But why?"

"There are plenty of rumours in circulation. Take your pick."

Harry raised his eyebrows and deep tramlines appeared on his weathered forehead.

"Like what?" he said.

"Oh, that he was having private acting lessons and was advised that he couldn't act half way through them; that he's having a breakdown; that he has..." I censored that one, but I saw the look of recognition in Harry's eye. I ran on quickly. "And seeing as it was mostly his money going into the show, an estimated three million, without him there's no show."

"But you had a contract, didn't you? Can't you sue them?"

"That's what Hélène said," I laughed. "But as I told her, theatre is a weird place. Different rules. And nobody likes to sue a management – you could get a bad name and then you'd never work again."

I could feel the bitter anger rising in my blood as I repeated the story to my father. For the third time in

36

my life, a job in the West End had been plucked from my grasp, and once again I was flagellating myself with the injustice of it. In a perverse way, I was enjoying the self-torture. Painful as it was to have been thwarted yet again, I needed to prod that pain, rekindle it, at every opportunity. It was the only connection I felt with my profession at all. I was like an abused child, who learns to prefer beatings to neglect.

"You should have complained," said Harry.

"Complain? You can't make waves like that," I said. "You might as well walk around with Trouble Maker tattooed on your forehead." I shook my head. "No. They've got us just where they want us, I'm afraid. A bunch of acquiescent sheep with as much clout as a wet cigar."

Harry had been staring at me throughout with his bush-baby eyes, shiny as half-sucked sweets. When I finished he seemed smaller, deflated.

"So there's no job?"

"No job," I repeated, as if I were in a language class, eagerly reproducing his tone of voice and pronunciation.

"I'm sorry about that," Harry said in a brittle, cheerful tone. "You don't seem to have much luck, do you?"

"Put it this way, dad. If it wasn't for bad luck, I wouldn't have any luck at all."

Harry laughed, then. He tilted back his head and let out a throaty chuckle, his stubbly chin lending him the aspect of a raucous Greek fisherman. I looked at him across the table, disconcerted. This is my parent, I thought, and I don't understand him. I can't read his moods. What makes him laugh? What makes him shout? Once again I was awed by the task ahead, the sheer glass mountain which rose before me, devoid of features or hand-holds. And once negotiated, my destination would be nothing more splendid than a hole in the ground, a cold hollow in which to sink the memory of my father. These morbid thoughts were thrown off-kilter by my father's continuing laughter. Laughter I hadn't heard for years. As I listened to it now I was struck, for the first time, by how like my own laugh it was. Clean yet grating, like a shiny saw biting through soft wood.

After I'd persuaded Harry to eat a banana, we returned to the sitting room and watched tv for a while – soap operas and game shows that I had never seen, and situation comedies in which all the stars were in their sixties. Harry's alarm went off just before the news, heralding a major administration of drugs from the extensive collection which huddled on his desk like malevolent toys.

As he shuffled over and began to unscrew various bottles, rattling pills into his dry, waiting palm, I thought about those clever pill boxes – the ones divided into compartments, one for each day of the week, subdivided still further into particular doses – which opened automatically at the appropriate hour, and wondered if my father would like one.

"Do you know what you're doing with those?" I asked him.

"It's all written down somewhere," he said in a grey voice. And as I looked at him, standing over the desk like a withered autumn leaf, I could see how tired he was.

Harry was sixty-eight years old and had, until very recently, enjoyed perfect health, a small yet robust physique, and surprising strength and stamina. At sixty he could still out-walk me. Now his skin had lost that hardy, outdoor quality, his face was set in a mask of unbending sufferance, and merely breathing had become a conscious effort. I had the impression that this diminutive man, my father, was no longer filling up his entire body. There were spaces in it – spaces carved by illness of the most insidious kind.

After several glasses of water, to wash down his evening pills, Harry turned his weary eyes on me.

"I'm tired, Fy," he said. "I think I'm ready to go up to bed."

"Okay."

We left the sitting room and walked down the long dark corridor, then on through the dining room, and came to the stairwell, where we paused for Harry to catch his breath. As the stair was built into a turret, there was no bannister, just a sheer face of twisting wooden treads rising between a cold outer wall and a crumbling central stone column. The stairs were still carpeted with leftover scraps of material that I had begged from the carpet shop in Norwich some twenty-three years before, and carried home in plastic bags with great excitement. The colourful crazy-paving effect, which my mother and I had tacked to the stairs with such bounteous care, had faded into dusty sepia tones through the years and had now achieved subtle, pastel shades more restful to the eye than their original garish hues.

"Do you want a hand up the stairs?" I offered, my voice tentative. I was worried that the suggestion might provoke another outburst.

"I can manage," Harry replied, setting his jaw at a defiant angle, and he set off up the stairs, letting out a tiny grunt of effort with each step.

Harry did not mount the stairs in the conventional manner. He went one step at a time, always leading with his right leg, always pausing before taking the next step. As I watched him climb the stair in that laborious fashion I was washed by a cleansing wave of pity, and stepped up to his side.

"Lean on me," I said.

I was the same height as my father, and as he draped his left arm around my neck and braced himself against the wall with his right, I realised that I was looking into the future. This was how *I* would be thirty five odd years from now. Frail, grey-haired, with character lines etching a once wholesome face, rendering it a cartoon caricature. I felt my father's bird-like chest beneath my arm as I helped him up to his room, and wondered at his transformation. This was the man who, as recently as a year ago, could rein-in the strongest, hottest of horses with his sinuous arms. Now he had trouble climbing stairs.

On the threshold of his bedroom, we paused. We looked at one another, both embarrassed by the enforced intimacy of our ascent. It was a tacit acknowledgement that I would be doing more intimate things for him before long, and neither of us felt comfortable with it.

"You'll be sleeping next door," said Harry, indicating the room that I had slept in as a child. "I'm sure I shan't need anything, but..."

"That's what I'm here for," I reminded him.

Harry nodded. "Goodnight, Fy," he said.

"Goodnight," I echoed. Turning in early tonight would do me no harm.

It was only then, as I walked back down those familiar stairs, that I realised Harry had been calling me Fy all day, and I immediately resented it. It was the legacy of my childhood, of being the youngest. I'd been christened Philip, which I hated for its middle-class pretensions, but the diminutive Fy – an elongation of the first syllable of my name – was execrable. I called myself Pip. All my friends called me Pip. I had ceased to hear the name Fy at an early age.

It was Rob who mentioned it, after thirty-two years of my not noticing.

"They all call you Fy," he'd said, the first time he met my sister and her family.

I didn't believe him and actually argued over it. "I'm sure I'd notice if they didn't call me Pip or Philip," I said.

But Rob was right.

Fy was appalling – not a name at all, just a sound – and since Rob had made me aware of it, I'd trained my sister to call me Pip. Even so, I was always on edge at family gatherings, waiting for that hideous bleat which was supposed to be my name. As I went outside to collect my bags from the car, I decided to ask Harry to call me Pip in future too, but a part of me already knew I wouldn't in the same way as I had failed to ask him to pay me for the groceries I'd bought earlier. It was impossible. He was the parent and I was the child. Some things were immutable.

On my way back to the house, I stood in the garden and was amazed by the completeness of the rural darkness. It would have been a perfect night for Kate – cloudless and full of stars. Half an hour later, I was settled in a chair with a cup of coffee, reading a book, when the phone rang in the hall. Groggily, I went to answer it. A preprogrammed response tumbled out of my mouth as I lifted the receiver.

"Hello Pip," said Hélène, the rough edges of her voice smoothed out by wine. "I promised to phone on your first evening, so here I am. And by the way, you just quoted your own number, not dad's."

"Yes, probably. I wasn't thinking," I mumbled.

"So how's it going?" she said.

"Not too bad, I think. Okay." I stared at the old fashioned barometer which hung on the wall opposite. The needle was pointing to FAIR WEATHER. "He's so *small*, Hélène. I could break him over my knee."

"Hmm. But he's not being a prickly sod?"

"Not really. He threw a tantrum over dinner, but I think

41

that was a blip. He seems rather quiet, in fact."

"This is the first time you've seen him since he went Happy Clappy, isn't it?" my sister mused.

"Mmm."

"Strange, isn't it? What you might call vacant possession."

I laughed. "It gives me the creeps. I keep expecting something – I don't know, something recognisable – but all I see is an uncanny, virtuous schoolboy."

"I know. I can't handle it at all. It makes me want to slap him, shake some sense into him. It looks so phoney."

I heard her take another sip of her drink. I could visualise her so well, sitting on her plush sofa by the open fire, her legs curled beneath her as she reclined, with the phone cradled between her chin and shoulder, leaving her hands free to flip through a magazine.

"How's Ewan and the kids?" I said.

"We're all fine," Hélène said. There was a pause. "So you're okay then?"

"I think so. But it's only my first day," I said. "You will come up and see me sometime, won't you?"

"I certainly will, Miss West."

"Good. Love to Ewan. And the kids."

"Mmm," Hélène said, sounding distracted. "And give me a ring if Harry gets snitty."

"Okay."

"Good night, little brother."

"Good night, 'Lène."

I replaced the reciever, then decided to ring my answering machine. I waited whilst my own voice told me that I wasn't there, then I gave the command for the messages to play back, a single mournful electronic bleep from a tiny black handset that I carried with me at all times. I didn't expect any messages, of course. I'd told all relevant people that I would be away, and had given my agent my number at Ravencrag so that he could call me directly if he needed to. But somebody had left a message – quite a long one – and I knew at once that it had to be Callum. I listened, half irritated and half amused, as his familiar light brogue rolled round his words, half melting them with sounds that could not be transcribed, whilst busy pub sounds filtered in from the background.

"Hello, Pip. I know you're not there because you're up in that fucking castle with that shit-for-brains father of yours..." There was the sound of heavy breathing for a few moments before he spoke again. This time his voice was full of pain. "Why didn't you give me your dad's number, Pip? You want to get away from me, don't you? I only want to talk to you for Christ's sake..." More heavy breathing. "Because I'm missing you, Pip. I know it's only a day, but I'm missing you. I fucking love you, you bastard. Don't know why. It's not as if you give me any hope. But then, last night..."

At this point the words became indistinct. Callum must have turned away from the phone. In the background there was distant thumping, and a muffled voice shouting something I couldn't catch. I made out the words 'hurry up', 'half an hour' and 'doorman' in the general wash of sound, but couldn't tell who was speaking. Then came the unmistakable sound of somebody kicking at a door and the line went dead. With a sigh, I bleeped my machine again, rewound the message tape and hung up, then went up to my childhood bedroom.

Once inside, I lay on the bed, experimenting with the mattress. It wasn't too bad, although it sagged somewhat in the middle, which restricted my movement and was like lying in a narrow, shallow grave. But I could live with that. I'd slept in much worse, in digs on tour – back in the days when I used to get work.

When I slipped between the sheets, I discovered that they were furry, thick and hot. At once, I sat up and stripped the blankets off the bed, knowing that I would not sleep well if I overheated. Satisfied with my environment, I settled down for the night, but despite my fatigue, the stresses of the day would not allow sleep. I was exhausted, but my mind was still running free over the events of the day, picking them up and examining them from new angles, like a jeweller studying the facets of a diamond.

Callum: The more he clung to me, the more he phoned or pitched up on my doorstep, the more he said he loved me, the greater was my desire to cut free of him. Why was that? It wasn't as if I was flooded with offers from other eligible men. And of course he was right about my escape to Ravencrag. I *was* trying to get away from him here; I had deliberately witheld Harry's number. I was hoping that somehow a change of environment without Callum's constant presence, often uninvited, would offer a new perspective on him, on myself, on our relationship – or whatever the hell it was we were supposed to be doing. I had no space to think in London, and I was sick to death of all the conflicting 'advice' I had received from my friends about it: *Ditch him* (Chris). *Define your boundaries* (Paul – ex lover). *Give him a chance* (John). All I knew was that I liked his company, except when he drank too much, and was happy to see him once or twice a week. I didn't think we had enough in common to sustain a more intense relationship than that. The problem was, Callum did. And he was in love with me. Sadly, in all the welter of uncertainty, there was one thing of which I was certain. I was not in love with him. So why didn't I have the strength to end it?

And Harry: How was I going to cope with him on a day

to day basis? What could cement the gaping fissures in our relationship and make the coming weeks even remotely tolerable for either of us? Why on earth had I agreed to come? And what would happen if a job came up in the meantime?

I offered these unanswerable questions to the dark night, where they hung above my head like a smothering blanket. Hours seemed to go by. I turned over and over, lying on my side, on my back, and then on my stomach; I grew hot, and a light patina of sweat broke out on my chest and forehead. I began to worry that if I didn't go to sleep immediately I'd be a wreck in the morning; I began to wonder if I should admit defeat and get up to read a book. It was a cycle I'd often experienced the night before a big audition, and I supposed that my current situation was not dissimilar in some respects. We'd both be performing for one another over the coming weeks, to some degree.

With that, my mind lurched into overdrive, freshly torturing me with the fiasco surrounding *Top Withins* – yet another job that had been offered with one hand and taken from me with another. My father's words this evening over dinner echoed in my mind as I lay there seething. *You don't seem to have much luck, do you?* I couldn't help but smile.

Good luck. That's what it took in my business, but I hadn't had very much of it in the twelve years I'd been acting. I'd had some *bad* luck, of course, such as the other time I'd managed finally to be cast in a West End musical, only to discover that the actor I was due to replace had decided to renew his contract at the last possible moment; or the time I was in the original regional cast of a play that transferred to the West End without me; or the time I'd been cast in a major touring show, and turned up at first rehearsal to be told that a mistake had been made: It wasn't me they wanted, but another actor. Our cvs had been mixed up at the auditions. True, these things were standard in the arena of theatre – I heard about them all the time – but when it actually happened to me I took a very long time to recover. I was never good at taking the knocks. The rejection seemed personal.

Knocked, dented, beaten almost into submission. That was me. I'd been lucky at first, on leaving drama school, too lucky perhaps, but after that initial short-lived roll my career had been a litany of frustration, disappointment and dole cheques. At drama school, we had been taught that theatre was not about working but about *not* working, and with the benefit of hindsight I could only agree. Unfortunately for me, I never quite negotiated my way around that particular frustration. It was my bête noire, the demon that ripped at my innards when I lowered my guard for even an instant. I was forever tormented by an overwhelming sense of uselessness.

Emotionally, I was not well equipped for a life in the grubby little business people call theatre, but still I persisted in it, because it wasn't a rational choice. I was infected with the actor's disease. It propelled me through the disappointments with vain promises that it would be my turn next time; it fuelled me with enormous ambition; and it made it impossible for me to give up, long after any normal person in any normal line of work would have capitulated on the grounds that it was leading nowhere, and turned their hand to something else. And there was no cure for this disease. I knew that I was never going to emulate my father and become a jockey, however much he wanted me to. I was stuck with the stinking, ignoble acting profession as surely as Charon was fated to row back and forth over the unappealing river Styx for all time.

Uncle Richard, my mother's brother, knew all about the actor's disease. He had it himself. I recalled how I'd once been to see him in a Tom Stoppard play at the Phoenix Theatre, when I was seventeen. At the time I was utterly in awe of him, and desperate to follow in his footsteps. He invited me into his dressing room after the show, gave me a tumbler full of neat gin which I didn't drink, stared at my insubstantial reflection in the light-bulb framed mirror and said, "So you want to be an actor?"

"Yes."

He began to remove his make up and shook his head.

"Don't," he said.

At the time I thought he was being grand and cynical, but now I could only concur. It was the only sensible piece of advice to give, because those who had the actor's disease would go out and become actors anyway, no matter what anybody said, and those who did not would be mercifully deterred.

Tossing in my bed, I sighed, awed by the prospect of spending another thirty years living on my nerves; always at the mercy of the fickle swing of fate's pendulum, or waiting for some magnanimous director to throw a crumb of work my way – which I probably wouldn't enjoy anyway. It wasn't much of a life. Why on earth did people think it was so glamorous?

By now, I'd worked myself into a state of tense wakefulness, and sleep seemed more remote than ever. Fortunately, I had expected to encounter occasions such as this during my stay – albeit not on my first night – and with that in mind I had brought my little red box along with me, which contained some good strong dope, some Rizlas, a couple of sleeping tablets, and an unidentified chubby white pill which Terry, a down-at-heel acquaintance of mine and sometime casual passer-on of drugs, had told me was E. I did not use any of these drugs regularly, but I was superstitious about always having some with me *in case* I wanted them. I liked the get-out clause they offered me – they were my security blanket against the rougher edges of life. Usually, I'd have no need of them, and my supply would last for months, or be offered around to friends, or more likely get lost, before I laid my hands on them. But I sensed that at Ravencrag they would come into their own.

I got the idea from a man named Mike, with whom I once travelled from London to Middlesborough by coach. Mike, an attractive grey haired man of about my father's age, was sitting next to me for the journey. Half way up the M1, the automatic door of our coach was wrenched free of its hinges, somehow, and clattered to rest some hundreds of yards behind us on the hard shoulder, like an outsized discarded hubcap. We, the disgruntled passengers, were to be transferred to another bus, which took more than two hours to arrive. In the meantime I sat on the broken-down bus, growing hotter and more bored as the minutes ticked by. I had nothing with which to occupy myself, not so much as a magazine, and could only look on in undisguised jealousy as my handsome neighbour, Mike, produced from his bag a novel, some chocolate, a drink, and finally a sandwich, which he proceeded to eat, absently, as he read his book. When he noticed my looks of longing, he leant towards me and offered me not food, but advice.

"My greatest fear is to be stuck somewhere without anything to read, anything to eat, or any chocolate. So I always take some with me," he said.

These words seemed so wise and true, as I sat sweltering in the brassy afternoon sun, that I never forgot them. Some years later, I added my own personal requirement to his list, namely drugs, and my superstitious habit was born.

I smiled, remembering Mike, but was seized by a

sudden wash of embarrassment as I recalled how I had pressed my thigh against his as I sat next to him, pretending to look out at the stream of passing traffic but all the time studying his face, reflected in the coach window. The ghost of his well groomed aquiline head had floated along beside me for miles, suspended above the fast lane, apparently oblivious to the erotic fantasies taking place in my young brain. Later, I was disturbed to realise that he bore some passing resemblance to Harry, my pugnacious father.

I got out of bed, rummaged in my bag, and located the box. Then I extracted a sleeping pill and blessed the god of Benzodiazapines from afar as I waited to spiral into a dreamless catatonia.

My days settled into a routine at Ravencrag. They were dull, sombre days of low skies and silence, where I sat in the living room with my father for hours on end without speaking. I hardly dared make noise of any kind, retreating into the role of diffident child against my will, and buried myself in books. I'd brought a stack of classic novels with me in anticipation of such days, novels I was too ashamed to admit I hadn't read, and proceeded to wade through them with little satisfaction, although I took perverse pleasure in managing to finish them, one by one.

Most of the time I felt somewhat redundant. Harry didn't like me fussing around him. On my first full day as his carer, he had forbidden me even to ask him how he was feeling.

"Stop hovering at my elbow, Fy," he said. "If I want your help, I'll ask for it." His tone was calm, but his face, and his sneering mouth, took on a cruel twist as he spoke.

People say that by the age of forty you have the face you deserve, and as I regarded Harry, blurting out this order in his new zombie voice, I knew that for him, at least, it was true. He was a proud, arrogant man, and looked it. A lifetime of bitterness at fate's unjust hand when it pushed him from his mount at the last fence, only yards away from winning the Gold Cup, breaking his collarbone and leg as it did so, had etched itself into every line and soaked into every pore. His leg had mended badly after the fall and he had never raced again. From then on, his face had let everyone know that he felt the world owed him.

"Just tell me if you want anything," I said.

Silence.

"That's why I'm here, dad. That's why you asked me to come."

I winced as I said this; we both knew it wasn't true. The truth was that in a moment of weakness, Harry had been pressured by Dr Daniels to phone not me, but Hélène, to ask for help. He had wanted her to come and be with him, the way she had nursed Kate all those years before. He had wanted the comfort of a woman's touch. If he had known, as he made that call, that it would not be his big, blonde, successful daughter who was to be his nurse, but his disappointing homosexual son, then he might not have bothered. But the call had been made, the plea for help uttered, and now I was here, reinhabiting the dark house after an absence of almost twelve years, negotiating silences as huge and unscalable as the mountains from which the Swiss cuckoo clock, upon which my gaze was now fixed, had come.

The pattern of our days continued, like a complex slow-dance. We would get up, I would prepare us a meal, make up the fire in the Norwegian stove, and then we would sit in the sitting room, reading. I might ask Harry if he wanted to go for a walk, but he would always refuse. Even the prospect of gazing on his beloved horses could not lure him from the safety and comfort of his chair. It was almost as if he had given up on life, and had decided to wait patiently in the sitting room for death to come and tap him on the shoulder. So I went out alone, taking short walks around the paddocks as respite from our forced proximity. On my second day, I'd sought out Arthur and said hello, as Harry had suggested, but Arthur had seemed uncomfortable with my presence, and I had not visited him again.

The first week of my vigil wafted over me like a miasma, and I felt out of time, as if I was taking part in a bad psychological thriller by Hitchcock, in which my father had been kidnapped, brainwashed, and returned as a flawless doppelganger. At every turn Harry surprised me with weird religious phrases, muttering lengthy, complicated benedictions over his food before eating, and ejaculating "Praise!" in a strange, ethereal voice at odd moments, for no particular reason. And he kept smiling his twisted smile. Hélène was right, I thought, as I observed him through the days, studying him as an ornithologist might study some rare and exotic bird. It did seem phoney. He was like a method actor rehearsing for a part. I kept expecting him to straighten up, stretch, flash a crooked grin at me and exclaim, "Bugger me, that's hard work!" But he never did.

On the fifth day, unable to bear the atmosphere in the house any longer, I offered to take him for a drive somewhere.

"No thanks. But you can take me to church on Sunday," he said, launching one of his crooked smiles.

Now it was Saturday afternoon, the sixth day of my visit, and once again, we were ensconced in our respective armchairs by the fire, reading our books. Today, however, I found that I couldn't concentrate. My mind was too full of my father. Already I had begun to search Harry for signs – signs of his failing health. Was he getting slower? Was he sleeping more than before? I couldn't tell. Perhaps his voice, or his breathing, was weaker, or was that simply age? I didn't know what I was looking for, or why I was looking, but I had a sneaking feeling that, subconsciously at least, I was calculating how long I was liable to be here, how long it would be before I could return to my own life. The fact was, I had come to Ravencrag to watch over my father whilst he died. That was incontrovertible. In the light of that, a part of me wished he'd just get on with it.

I let *Martin Chuzzlewit* fall face down into my lap, and looked at my father, asleep in his armchair. His head was resting against the wing of the chair, crunching his face up like a rubber doll's mask. When he woke, he would have a deep crease in his cheek, from eyebrow to chin, like a war wound.

Whilst his eyes were closed, it was safe for me to feel tenderly towards him, a tenderness engendered not because he was my father, but because he was ill. His smallness, the caste of his once-handsome face, the little round glasses – in danger of slipping from the end of his nose as his face fell forward – all tugged at my heart and made me want to kiss him. I was surprised at the violence of the feeling, and still more surprised to find myself rising from my chair to walk across the room.

Unsure of my motives, I crossed to where he was sitting, and stood beside my sleeping father, listening to the rasp of his breath as a parent might stand in a bedroom doorway, listening to the placid breathing of a child in the darkened room beyond. Slowly, I bent down towards Harry's face, my lips puckered for the planting of a kiss. A compassionate kiss from a healthy man to a sick one. But as my face descended, and a moment before my lips made contact with his warm and untroubled brow, Harry opened his eyes. I was unable to stop myself now, caught as I was in the momentum of the movement, and so I planted the kiss on his head and withdrew. My father's eyes, as I stepped away from him, were full of such terror, such incomprehension, that my skin grew clammy in an instant. It was not a look of hate, just the look of one who is unable to accept.

"What are you doing?" he said in a gluey voice.

"Nothing. I... I don't know," I said, and stepped away still further, as if he might leap up and hit me, as he had done so frequently when I was a child.

Harry raised a hand to his forehead, and felt the place where I had kissed him, as if he expected it to be wet with saliva. Then he fixed me with a stare.

"What did you kiss me for?" he demanded. His tone was bewildered, petulant.

"I just wanted to," I said. I couldn't tell him that he'd looked so vulnerable, asleep in his chair, that I'd been unable to stop myself; that despite everything, I'd wanted to kiss him. The words I needed did not exist in any language.

"Did you think I was dead?"

"Of course not."

"Well, I'm not dead. Not yet," he said.

"I know."

There was a tight pause, fractured by the whine of a small aircraft overhead. We looked at one another as it droned past like a giant, morose wasp, and in that moment I realised that we had no point of contact. The bridge between us was Kate, but she had left us to flounder on alone. We were like two shipwrecked men, Harry and I, stranded on neighbouring desert islands, just visible to one another across an unnavigable, treacherous sea. Neither of us knew semaphore, so we could not communicate. And anyway, what was there to say? Feeling angry, disappointed and rejected, I turned and left the room without a word.

All at once I needed to get out of the house, to escape the oppression of my father's eyes. So desperate was I to escape, I almost ran up the corridor and soon found myself in the coat room. As I pulled on my jacket and left the house I was aware that I was trembling. It was not until the front door shut behind me with a weighty, definitive thump that I relaxed at last, and stood in the garden, breathing the winter air into my lungs like a man saved from drowning.

It was a still, dull afternoon, and the air was chilled by a low, steely sky. I pulled my coat tight about my throat as I walked around the side of the house and let myself out of the garden, then stood on the driveway, deciding which way to go. To the right lay the stable yard with its little wooden clock tower, and beyond that there were paddocks and parkland; to the left was the driveway leading back out to the road, flanked by more paddocks. I selected this route, and walked beneath the gothic archway which bestrode the drive, and looked up at its shadowy, vaulted ceiling, complete with cornices and piping. In each corner was a grimacing gargoyle, reminding me of the past summers of my childhood, when swallows nested in their open mouths, and I would run out each morning before school to see if the fledglings were ready to fly. Looking up at them now, bereft of their avian tenants, I was struck by how much one of them resembled my father as he slept, squashed-faced, in his wing chair. The recognition made me laugh out loud, but the sound soon died in my throat.

What was it that I had seen in Harry's eyes as my lips touched his small, dry head? A look of distrust, an inability to connect. I wondered if it been like that for Kate. Had she lived her married life reaching out for Harry, trying to find the love she knew must be there, enfolded in some secret corner of his heart, yet always recoiling empty-handed? I tried to remember them together, dredging my memory for a moment that I could point to and say, Yes! Look there! He loves her! But there were none. He certainly never touched or kissed her in my presence – he never kissed any of us. Perhaps his love for Kate was reserved for private moments; perhaps it was only expressed behind closed doors. I very much wanted to believe that, but I was certain it wasn't true. For if so, why was he always out at the races, or riding horses, or in some bar or other, leaving her to turn her sad face up to the stars, feeling closer to Andromeda than she did to him?

I knew it had been too much for Rose. Rose, his second wife, who had only stayed two years. Harry had married her within six months of burying Kate, an undignified, hasty conjugation which scalded the hearts of my sister and me, hearts still smarting from the loss of our mother. Rose was a nice enough woman, placid, like Kate, but without the sparkle, the flair, or the wit that our mother had possessed, and I couldn't bring myself to like her. She was not my mother, and I didn't want her there. She tried to love Harry, and to accept us, her grown up step-children, but each time I saw her she seemed more weary, more distant. When she'd realised that Harry was only looking for a replacement for Kate, some woman to cook, clean and coddle, she had decided to get out. If the look I'd just seen in Harry's eyes was any indication, she'd made the right choice. There was granite in those eyes – cold, hard, impermeable rock.

Now, there were no mementoes of Rose's stay at Ravencrag, as if Harry wished to expunge the memory from his mind. Not a single trinket or photograph remained. Those two years had been excised from his life with the precision of a surgeon, and time had sealed up around the wound, denying it, as if the unhappy episode had never taken place.

Rose had not managed to make any lasting impression on the house because the walls themselves had resisted her presence. When she left, Harry removed all the pictures she'd hung, consigning them to dustbins or drawers; he returned all the furniture, which she had painstakingly rearranged, to their previous stations about the house – locations Kate had chosen for them, where they still stood, like a museum to her memory. It was easy to believe that Rose had never existed. For two years of her life she had tried to make a home here, yet no shred of evidence survived. Although I had resented Rose as a step-mother, I was glad that she would never know of this final rejection.

But why did Harry wish to forget her so completely? I shook my head and walked on. It was another of those unknowable things about my father, and I doubted that I would ever come to understand it.

As I walked further from the house, and from Harry, I grew calm. I let the silence of the parkland lap over me as I climbed the wooden fence of the nearest paddock and crossed it, diagonally, heading for the beech forest beyond, now sparse-looking and angular, like an X-ray in reverse against the white sky. Looking ahead, I noticed that my projected path would take me right through a knot of horses milling together a few yards away. They stood with their heads low to the ground, white dragon breath puffing from their noses as they nibbled at the dead grass, their forelegs at casual angles, like men drinking at a bar. As I approached, they lifted their large, languid heads and stared at me with their black eyes, their flanks twitching, and for a moment I was transported by their tranquil, natural beauty, and their leathery animal smell, so much like sex. Then the nearest one turned and presented me with its muscular, conker-shiny backside, raised its tail, and defecated copiously at my feet, and with that the spell was broken. These were not ethereal beasts after all, but glorified farm animals. I hurried on through them and they stepped back, blinking, nodding, unsure of this stranger in their midst. No doubt they had thought I might be Arthur, coming to lead them back to the warmth of their stalls.

I left the horses behind me, heard the diminishing sounds of lips tearing at grass, and the occasional tinkle of a loose buckle on a New Zealand rug as I pressed on towards the trees. The sleeping beech wood smelt of mulch and decay as I slipped beneath its eaves, and the trees closed around me, protecting me from the weight of the sky. Slowly, I meandered along the dark wet paths, scuffing through layers of dead brown leaves with my hands deep in my pockets. Here, amongst these tall, somnolent beeches, I felt quite alone for the first time since my arrival at Ravencrag. I had seldom, if ever, walked through End Wood on my own, and this exaggerated the isolation I felt within. But it was not my father that I missed as I circumvented the house – describing an almost perfect circle around Ravencrag and the parkland belonging to it in the endless curve of End Wood – for he had never been out walking with me. Nor was it the dogs, who used to accompany me when I felt the need for escape, when Kate was busy. It was my mother herself. I wanted her to be walking with me now, with that rolling gait of hers, pointing out fungi and small plants, and telling me their names.

The veined, neon-green beech leaves stretched overhead, layer upon layer, muffling everything and blocking out the summer sun. Behind us and before us, the dogs thundered to and fro, sniffing frantically at the trunks of trees, running after imagined squirrels, bouncing up against our legs with large muddy paws and slack-tongued dog grins. Kate and I were silent as we walked, our sloth counterpointing the manic activity of the four dogs – large, stupid pointers with big hearts and doe eyes, who loved us unreservedly.

We had left the house smouldering beneath a pall of acrimony. I had dared to criticize my father as he slouched, glassy eyed, in front of the racing from Doncaster, for not taking Kate into Bruxley for the afternoon. Apparently, this was unforgivable.

"You shouldn't have said that, Pip," my mother told me as we ambled through the cool woods. "You shouldn't talk to him like that."

"Why not?" I cried. I was eighteen and tempestuous, quite certain that everything was either black or white. "He is selfish."

Kate sighed, and shot me a sideways look. "But it's not the kind of thing that you can say," she replied.

"Even if it's true?"

Kate drew in an annoyed breath and called the dogs, who had strayed too far away from us and had receded to tiny white dots amongst the darkness of the trees. Her call was impressively loud and penetrating, a wordless ululation to which they had learned to respond. It crashed between the trunks of the silent trees like floodwater.

I pressed on with my point as the dogs bounded towards us, ears flapping. "You must agree that it's true?" I said. "What other explanation is there? Why else would he refuse?"

Kate could not drive, and I had not yet learnt. We lived ten miles from Bruxley, and without Harry to drive her there, Kate had to walk the length of the drive, something over a mile, and wait for one of the infrequent, and often cancelled, buses. The trip could easily take most of the day. I felt sorry for my mother, marooned here in our strange house amongst my father's horses. For someone like Hélène, Ravencrag was a paradise – miles of parkland, a gallop, and some practice brush fences bordering End Wood – but Kate, like me, was not touched by the magic of horses, and consequently life here was something like a prison sentence. There was a limit to country walking, and reading. At least I had my bike and could cycle off to visit friends, or make the occasional trip into Norwich. Kate did not have this advantage, and was trapped.

"He's got to do the horses," Kate said. The statement was bald, blunt, and sounded as unconvincing now as it had when Harry had said it, through those downward-curling lips of his.

"He doesn't do them until the evening. You know that," I said. "And anyway, Arthur could always do them, or I could."

Kate stopped walking and looked at me. We both knew that I hadn't done the horses, or offered to, for almost a year. Not since the famous row I'd had with Harry over Jasper, the horse bought for myself and Hélène. I hadn't so much as led a horse out to grass, let alone groomed, mucked out, or exercised one, in the intervening period.

I smiled and shrugged. "I would," I said.

"Why don't you, then?"

"I mean, I would for you. If it meant you could get away for the day."

We walked on. Dappled light danced at our feet as the dogs massed around us, checking up on us, making certain we were following before racing off again, with tiny clods of earth flying out behind them.

"He wants you to, you know," said Kate.

"What?"

"He wants you to ride again." My mother's tone was affectionate, full of smile.

"Then why doesn't he ask me to?"

"Because he's Harry," my mother sighed. "Because he has to

be right. But that doesn't mean he doesn't want you to."

"I don't care," I said. "He told me I couldn't ride any more, and that's that." My face closed of its own volition, becoming rigid as a gravestone, and inviolable. "And I'm not interested in riding if there are strings attached."

"He knows that, Pip," Kate said. "There won't be any conditions. Why don't you ask him?"

But Harry and I had been engaged in our head to head battle for too long now – too long to be able to stop: He wouldn't allow me to ride if I wasn't prepared to work in the yard as well, and I, for my part, refused to ride if my duties involved anything more than tacking up. This infuriated Harry and I knew it. It was my greatest weapon against him, and easy to wield because it was no great sacrifice for me to forgo riding. Harry, of course, had not realised this. He had simply referred to his own all-consuming passion for horses, and had imagined that I must feel the same. He thought that I was being bull-headed. It was an impasse in which I, tacitly at least, held the upper hand. Any sort of retreat or truce at this stage would be impossible.

"No," I said. "I'm never going to ride again."

Quite suddenly, Kate stepped off the path, leant back against the trunk of a large copper beech, and began to cry. She tilted her head back, the way she always did when she was star-gazing, the way Hélène did, and let the tears roll down her dark cheeks without a sound. I stood on the path, motionless, unsure what to do. I had never seen my mother cry before, and I had imagined that when the time came I would see Kate, so expansive with her other emotions, emitting loud sobs with heaving shoulders – not this calm, silent overspilling of hurt which stopped my heart. It was the strangeness of it which stilled me.

I walked over to her and put my hands on her shoulders. "What's the matter?" I said.

She looked at me with moist eyes. "Why do you hate him?" she said.

Hate was such a strong, unequivocal word that it made me shudder. I certainly did not hate my father, and I wondered where the idea came from. It was true that I did not respect Harry for his behaviour, nor did I agree with him very often, but I did not hate him. Hate required boundless energy, and I needed to keep all mine for myself, in order to find my way out of the labyrinth of my own feelings, which had multiplied around my heart like strange fungus over the previous two years. So far, each exit had been blocked by the naked bodies of boys.

"I don't hate him," I smiled. Our faces hung close together beneath the canopy of plum coloured leaves.

"Harry thinks you do. He keeps saying, 'I know he hates me, I know he hates me'. Of course I tell him you don't, but..."

"That's stupid."

Kate sighed out a ragged breath, which played across my face like a sirocco from Africa. "So why do you argue all the time?" she said.

Throughout our childhood, Harry had either been absent or he had shouted at us, or hit us. But as children we had never responded. It was only after we moved to Ravencrag, and my sister finally fled, leaving me alone with him, that I began to shout back. I had a lot of scores to settle, a lot of shouting to do. I had to shout for myself, for Hélène, and also for Kate, who never said a word, who soaked it all up like a sponge.

"I don't know," I said.

Kate looked at me hard, studying every detail of my face as if she was about to paint it.

"But it's always been you, hasn't it, Pip?" she said. "First it was you and Hélène, now it's you and Harry."

She took my head in her hands and stared into my eyes, as if she might be able to see my soul inside if she looked hard enough.

"What's inside you that makes you like that? What's the matter with you?" she said. Her tone was soft, loving, and full of confusion.

I felt a tight constriction in my chest. I wanted to tell her that I couldn't bear to watch Harry be unfair to her, that I couldn't wait to escape the prison of Ravencrag forever, that if I never saw a horse again it wouldn't be soon enough – but the wood was too quiet, the light too bright, and the day had already been weakened by large events. I felt sure that it could not support the extra weight of my answer, so I said nothing.

At our feet, the dogs milled about listlessly, tilting their heads from side to side, their faces puckered by little frowns. They wanted to know why we had stopped.

"Come on," I said, moving back to the path, "we're worrying the dogs."

For a moment, Kate did not move. She remained with her back to the tree, and looked at me with a hint of a slow smile.

"You nearly told me, then," she said in a low voice. "Didn't you?"

The shrill call of a pheasant pierced the air, and I was released back into the still, winter wood. No dogs trotted at my heels now – they were long dead, and lay peacefully at the end of the garden, buried beneath the cherry trees. I stared down the empty path ahead, and sighed to myself as the present reclaimed me. Once again I was walking amongst the beeches, having fled the stifling atmosphere of the house to walk the endless loop of End Wood until I was ready to return to my father, to face him across the chasm which separated us. But now I was alone, and he was a different man. A frightened, dying man who smiled and prayed, not the bullying autocrat against whom I had pitted myself for all these years.

I walked on for some time, and arrived at the gallop, with its practice fences which rose almost to my shoulder. I smiled as I looked at those stiff, scratchy fences, remembering the times I'd cantered Jasper up to them and popped him over, pretending to be Harvey Smith. I never liked to gallop at them jockey-style, like Hélène, because I was too frightened. I could picture her now, standing in her short stirrups, leaning forward to the neck of her mount with an impossibly short rein, flying past me, arching over the fence, and galloping away whilst Harry nodded.

"She's not got your hands," he'd say. "She won't give him his head. Look at the length of that rein."

Hélène liked to ride on a tight rein, pulling Jasper's chin right under his neck, like a chess piece, whilst I would ride with my hands low like a cowboy, on a very long rein, and slap the side of his neck with the loose strap to indicate what I wanted him to do. Harry claimed that this was more difficult, but I did it only because it fitted my image of myself. I did not want to be a jockey, and I hoped that my flamboyant hacking style would demonstrate this.

"She's not got kind hands," Harry would say again as the sound of hooves diminished. "She needs to look at your hands." And I would be pleased at this approbation, doled out to me from my father, despite the fact that it was Hélène who wanted to race, not I. But already she was getting too big for that.

I cut through the wood and crossed the parkland, returning to the house from the opposite direction, and passed the yard and the clock tower, with its four small clock faces frozen at different times. Arthur was busy there, wheeling a barrow full of soiled straw towards the muck heap. He turned his ruddy, weather beaten face towards me as I went by, and raised an arm in salute.

"Hello there, boy," he said.

I stopped. "Hello," I said.

"I've not seen you round this way for a bit," he said. "How are you?"

"I'm all right," I said, forcing myself to smile. "Harry's been keeping me busy."

Arthur's face took on a leaden aspect. "Oh yes. Terrible business, isn't it? Terrible." He shook his head as he spoke, his eyes averted from me.

"Yes," I sighed. "Horrible."

"But, you know, I still don't understand it," said Arthur. "It's not like him at all."

My stomach clenched inside me. I had known Arthur since I was thirteen, when we'd first arrived at Ravencrag. He had been a friend and companion to me over the years, always ready with a smile, always willing to help me with the horses. It had been Arthur, not Harry, who had taught me to ride. I didn't want all that to end in ignorant statements about who could, or could not, be expected to contract Aids.

"What isn't like him?" I asked, growing wary.

Arthur looked at me with an expression of patient wonder, the expression he'd used when I'd been unable to tighten a girth, or fasten a head-collar. Tasks so simple that an idiot could perform them.

"All this God business," he told me, keeping his voice low. "All this Bless me Father for I have sinned."

I smiled, and chided myself for having thought badly of Arthur. He was a simple man and didn't indulge in moral judgement. "Oh, that," I said.

Arthur glanced about the yard, as if there might be spies hiding in the empty stalls, and leant towards me. "It's creepy, boy. Creepy," he said.

"Yes. It is a bit."

"And why? Thaa's what I want to know. What's the reason for it?"

I shrugged.

"But I'm glad you've come to keep an eye on him,

64

boy, and thaa's a fact," Arthur told me. "He's not been acting natural, lately. Not been hisself at all. Frightened me off, he has, ever since I found him that day lying out on the floor like that, with his mouth all open, and droolin' and gibberin' –"

Arthur must have seen a look of surprise settle on my face, because he stopped short, and looked at me.

"Haan't he told you all this, boy?" he added, his voice faltering.

"Not exactly."

Arthur coughed, clearly worried that he might have betrayed the confidence of his old friend.

"But thaa's why you've come, though?" he said, his deep-set eyes searching me. "To see he's all right, since he got this cancer and reckon he saw God?"

"I'm looking after him now, yes," I said carefully.

Arthur looked about him, at the yawning empty stables, then down at the barrow load of muck which had remained between us throughout our exchange.

"Lost all interest in the horses, even, he has," said Arthur, shaking his head. "Never thought I'd see that. Never!"

"God moves in mysterious ways," I said.

"Oh don't," said Arthur, waving me away with a sturdy arm and trying to ward off a smile. "Thaa's not funny, boy."

We looked at each other for a moment.

"I'd better get back to the house," I said.

"Right-o." Arthur picked up the barrow and began to wheel it away. "And if you want to try Delaware Gold," he added, shouting over his shoulder as I walked on, "just come lookin'. Sound as a pound he is now."

"Thanks," I said. "Perhaps I will."

As I walked back to the house, I mulled over what

Arthur had just said, and realised with a start that Harry had not told him the truth about his illness. Arthur was a man quite without side or guile. If he had known, he would have mentioned it. But he seemed only to be concerned about Harry's mental state since his conversion. This was worrying. Arthur was Harry's best friend, and if Harry had not confided in him, then it was certain that he would have told nobody else. This meant that he had never spoken about it, had been dragging his secret around with him like a vast, invisible weight for months. Perhaps this was a way in which I could actually be of use to Harry at last. He could talk to me, and I could listen. He would not have to confide in me, because I already knew, and that would make it easier. As I slipped back into the chilly house, I wondered how I could instigate such a conversation, and if it would be a good idea.

On entering the sitting room I found Harry asleep in his chair, seemingly in exactly the position he'd been in when I left the room an hour before. He woke when I sat down opposite him.

"Where have you been?" he said.

"I went to End Wood, through the paddocks," I said.

Harry shifted in his chair, blinking, waking up more thoroughly. "Which one?" he said.

"Primrose," I replied.

All the paddocks had names. I'd never known why, or who had invented them, but it was probably Kate. It was the kind of thing she did.

"The horses were in it," I added.

"Which horses?" Harry sounded like a petulant quizmaster.

"How on earth should I know?"

I tried to remember what the horses had looked like, but they all seemed more or less the same to me. Then I remembered the one that had raised its tail and defecated almost on my feet.

"There was a dark chestnut," I said. "Not very big, but strong, and incredibly glossy. A gelding."

"That's Delaware Gold," said Harry.

"He almost shat on me," I complained.

My father smiled. "Beautiful, isn't he? He's your sort of horse, Fy. You should try him."

"I haven't ridden a horse for twenty years, dad. I'd probably fall off and break my neck."

"He's not racing fit now. You could handle him," said Harry. He sat up in his chair, and leant forward. "I'd like to see you ride him, Fy. You were made for each other."

At Harry's words my flesh turned clammy, and the hairs on the back of my neck stood up. It was the first time that he had directly asked me to ride a horse in twenty years. He had not expressed any wish for me to do so since the fateful day that I had refused to fetch Jasper in from the paddocks, let my armful of tack crash to the concrete floor of the tack room, and stormed out of the yard in a fit of adolescent rejection of everything to do with horses. I remembered this acutely, because it happened two days after I first told my parents I was gay.

I looked at my father for a moment. "Maybe," I conceded.

And Harry smiled, because I had not said 'no'.

That evening, Harry developed a dry cough and sat in his wing chair hacking gently into a white hanky, with bowed shoulders. His already tiny appetite disappeared completely, and he went to bed at seven o'clock having eaten nothing. He was finding it difficult to breathe without coughing, and we shuffled through the house, to the foot of the stairs, even more slowly than usual.

I stood in the dark stairwell feeling awkward. I didn't

know whether or not to offer to assist him up the stairs. I didn't know whether or not I had been forgiven for the kiss that I had so injudiciously planted on his forehead earlier on. I watched, in an agony of indecision, as he hauled himself up the bottom stair, but the effort precipitated a bout of severe coughing and my decision was made.

"Come on," I said as I moved to his side, "let me help you."

"What are you doing, Fy? No, I can manage," Harry gasped, trying to get away from me. "Let me be."

Despite Harry's protest, I slipped my right arm behind his back and my left beneath his legs, and picked him up with ease. He weighed as little as a leaf as I held him in my arms, but his shrunken body remained rigid, like a bundle of sticks, as I mounted the stairs. It was hard to negotiate the endless curve of the staircase with him resisting me like this.

"Relax, dad," I said as I pushed open the door of his bedroom with my knee. "It's the easiest way."

Harry didn't look at me as I lowered his legs to the ground, just stared over my shoulder at a point on the wallpaper behind me. He sat down on the bed and coughed, an echoey sound like a voice bouncing from wall to wall in an empty room. It was dry as dust.

"Do you need anything?" I said. "Do you have any special medicine for that cough?"

"No. I've never had it before," said Harry, still not looking at me.

"I'll bring you some water."

When I returned from the kitchen, Harry was already in bed. I'd also brought him his book and his glasses, but he didn't want them.

"What about your pills?" I said.

"I've already taken them."

I looked at him for a long moment.

"I have!" he insisted.

"All right. I'll be next door if you want anything."

"But it's only seven o'clock, Fy. You can't go to bed yet."

"I'll be next door," I repeated. "Good night." And I left the room before he could say anything else.

The next morning, Sunday morning, Harry's cough was worse. The rasping dryness had gone, usurped by a more alarming wet, phlegmy rattle. He looked as if he'd slept badly, if at all, and there were dark bruises beneath his eyes. Nevertheless, he insisted on getting up and going to church, and could not be persuaded otherwise.

"You promised to drive me," Harry wheezed through his thin lips.

"I know, but that was before you got this cough," I told him. "We should call out Dr Daniels. You should stay in bed. It might be serious."

"But I want to feel Jesus," said Harry, countering my protests.

And I relented.

As I drove him to the Archangel Gabriel Baptist Tabernacle, following his directions, I felt my stomach tighten. I could see his illness claiming him, second by second, the way ink advances across blotting paper. Soon there would be no part of him that remained untouched and the blotting paper would be soaked through. I'd read this story before, too many times now, and I knew how it ended. The cough would turn into pneumonia, he would take to his bed, and then he would die. I was seeing the beginning of the end of Harry, and I just wasn't ready for it. It had slunk up on us when we weren't looking, as it always did.

The church was in Slyfold, and turned out to be a huge,

low, school-hall type building, which squatted like an abscess on the outskirts of this otherwise picturesque town. It was next to a field, which had been thrown open to be used as a car park for the faithful. A tortured Christ, spattered with bird droppings, hung from the wall above the church doors, but apart from that, there was no indication that this was a house of worship. There was no spire, no stained-glass windows, no graveyard. Just a large brick box with tiny windows high up.

I helped Harry to the door of the unappealing building. He clung to my arm with his tiny claw hands as he shuffled up the path, dressed in a suit for the first time that I could remember, and I felt like a father giving away his daughter at a wedding. Half way to the door we had to stop for him to cough – a sad, bubbling boom that was the sound of despair. As he lowered his starched white hanky from his mouth, I noticed a bright, bloody jewel of infected mucus glistening within, and I knew that the rebellion of his lungs had begun. I wondered what other vital functions inside him, belied by his still-perfect face, had decided to go AWOL in sympathy. I was sure he had begun his long descent into dust.

In the shade of the door, a smiling woman with frightening Margaret Thatcher eyes took my father from me and led him inside the church.

"I'll wait for you in the car," I said, and turned back down the path.

"Don't you want to feel Jesus?" Harry called after me in a voice like paper.

"I don't need him," I said, and returned to the car.

I watched, amazed, from the safety of the driver's seat as literally hundreds of people turned up to worship. Now I understood why the building was so large, and why this whole field had been given over as a car park.

70

But why was it here at all, in this small Norfolk town? Had somebody had a vision one day, a message from God telling them to build a church on this particular spot?

In a kind of shell shock, I watched the faithful gathering. I had always imagined followers of religion to be elderly women having an each way bet before they shuffled into the abyss, but these people did not fit that description at all. Most of them arrived in expensive company cars, sliding into the field with big, silent engines. They were nuclear families with smiling cardboard faces, lambent with moral rectitude and hypocrisy, and I cringed, feeling completely alien as I stared at them through my windscreen.

The service itself went on for more than two hours, and I wondered what they could be doing in there for so long. In all that time I did not hear a single hymn being sung, there were no enthusiastic tambourines or guitars, and there was no gospel choir. Instead there was a permanent mass muttering, like the groaning of a large building in a high wind.

At length, people began to spew back into the real world from the dark mouth of the church. They did not seem touched by God. But then I saw Harry, and I had to look twice, because at first I was sure it could not be him. He was standing straight, and was walking with a swing in his step, a lopsided smile blooming on his face. He looked ten years younger.

"Praise!" he said with a satisfied sigh as he let himself into the car and sat down. "That was powerful."

I looked at his shining face and my own faith, my devout atheism, faltered. Harry was not coughing at all.

"Shall we go?"

"There's too many people trying to leave just now," I said. "It'll be easier if we wait for a while. Let the road clear a bit."

"If you wish."

We sat in silence for a moment, and Harry drummed his fingers against his thin, suited leg to a tune playing in his head.

"You're looking well," I remarked.

"It's the Jesus in me, Fy. That's what you're seeing. Praise! And it was powerful today. We spoke in tongues. There were visions." He turned to look at me. "The pastor told me I was healed!"

"What did he think was wrong with you?" I said.

Harry didn't answer, but turned away and stared through the windscreen, and at once I wished I could unsay the words, reel them back into my mouth like an angler bringing in a fish.

"Well, whatever it is, you look good on it," I said.

But the light had already left his eyes, and the healthy flush drained from his cheeks as I watched. By the time I started the engine and made for home, he had begun to cough again, and I wondered at how dangerous simple words could be.

At tea time, I called Hélène. I was feeling responsible for Harry's relapse, and needed some support.

"Hello, little brother," she said in her loud, bright voice. "I've been feeling guilty because I haven't come up to see you, and I promised I would. My excuse is that I've got a major case on at the moment. How is everything?"

"Up and down," I told her. "I had to take Harry to church today."

"That must have been fun," my sister deadpanned.

"It was horrible," I said. "Actually, it was strange, 'Lène. He'd developed a terrible cough in the night, and then it went away when he went to church. But now it's back again."

"Of course it bloody is," Hélène said. "Coughs don't just

disappear."

"He said he had been healed."

"How very Christian Scientist of him," she said. Then, after a brief pause, she added, "What exactly *is* his religion, anyway?"

"I don't know. Some kind of Baptist fundamentalism, I suppose. I haven't asked."

"I don't blame you," Hélène said.

When I rang off, my mood had not improved.

Later in the day, however, Harry's cough disappeared once more. The hack diminished to a rattle, then to a sputter, before vanishing altogether like the quietening of the wind after a violent storm. The stillness which followed seemed more contained, more profound than before, and Harry could not stop smiling. The silence that hung between us now was not oppressive, but soothing. I allowed myself to relax a little. Perhaps this wasn't the end after all.

That night, Harry climbed the stairs to his bedroom unaided – albeit with painful slowness. He stood on the landing and smiled at me, his eyes bright with all the delight of a child who has just mastered the art of riding a bicycle.

"Praise the Lord!" said Harry as he opened the door to his bedroom. "I'm cured."

I smiled at him, but my heart was sad. I felt like a parent who knows he must soon tell his children that Father Christmas isn't real.

"Yes," I shrugged as I made off to my own room. "Why not?"

Some time later, I was disturbed from sleep by the distant telephone. In my experience, late night phone calls only heralded bad news, so it was with some trepidation that I fumbled my way down the dark spiral staircase, through the dining room and into the hall, where the profound coldness brought me out in goose bumps. I was fully awake at once.

"Hello?"

"Oh hi, babe, it's me."

"Callum!" I cried. "What's up?"

"Oh nothing. Just wanted to talk to you. You all right?"

My former anxiety immediately transmuted into anger. "You wanted to call me *now?* It's the middle of the night," I told him.

"Is it?"

"Yes. It is. What do you want?"

"Me? Nothin'." Callum hiccoughed, then let out a quiet, yet distinct, fart. "Jus' wanted to talk to you, that's all."

"You sound drunk."

"Maybe," Callum chuckled. "I've been out celebratin' with Chris and John."

Chris was an old friend of mine from drama school and John, his lover, was an old friend of Callum's. It was one of the ties that bound us together. Whatever happened, if I socialised with Chris I would always run into Callum. It was ineluctable. This was why I'd never succeeded in cutting Callum out of my life. He was destined to haunt me.

"Listen, Callum. I've had a lousy day and now you've woken me up. I'm glad you've had a good evening but really, I don't need this."

"D'you not want to know what I was celebratin'?"

I let out a curt, long-suffering sigh. "If I must."

"I won that competition I was tellin' you about. That one in the paper."

Callum bought lottery tickets, sent off for free draws, and entered competitions at every opportunity. It was a kind of compulsion with him. To my knowledge he'd never won so much as ten pounds.

"Congratulations. What have you won?" I asked him.

"A weekend break for two. You can go to Edinburgh, Glasgow, London, Manchester, or Bristol."

"That's great," I said. "Who are you going to take?"

Callum choked back a cry – of pain? rage? I wasn't sure – then cleared his throat. "Christ, you're a bastard, Pip," he drawled. "It's you I'm taking. I'm taking *you*!"

Now I felt guilty for being short with him. But I was also angry. This was familiar territory between me and Callum. "You do this deliberately, don't you!" I told him, raising my voice. "You're always setting me tests; tests that I can only fail. You *know* I can't come away with you. I'm looking after my father! You know that, yet still you ask. You *want* me to reject you."

Callum was silent.

"Look, I'm sorry," I told him. "It's late. I'm tired and stressed. Let's talk about this some other time."

"I love you, you bastard," Callum mumbled.

I responded with that famous, devastating line, "I know", then put the phone down. And it wasn't until I was back in bed that I thought to wonder how Callum had acquired Harry's ex-directory number at Ravencrag.

Days passed, but Callum didn't call again, about which I was pleased. Harry had begun to complain that too many people were ringing up, and the last thing I needed was for Callum to start pestering me, now that he had somehow found my phone number.

Harry, meanwhile, regained some strength. He ate his meals, and he slept less during the day. This was both good and bad. It was good, of course, that he was feeling better – I refused to use Harry's term, 'recovering', because I didn't believe it for a minute – but it did make our days awkward and difficult again. There we sat, in our respective chairs, staring into the Norwegian stove and thinking our separate thoughts. We did not speak. I tried to tell myself that our silence was unobtrusive, acceptable, but I could not quite chip away the embarrassment I felt, which had settled over me like a layer of cement. I found it inhibiting everything I did. I felt deficient, being unable to think of anything to say. Inadequate. When Harry had spent most of his days asleep, the silences had not seemed so sharp, so bright.

Slowly, I began to lose track of time at Ravencrag. Each day was so very much like the one before and the one after it that they telescoped into one another to form one huge, monotonous moment, like a permanently held breath, beneath the white Norfolk sky. I didn't know what day it was any more. I had delivered up my life to our silence, to our waiting, to my astonishment at his remission.

One such afternoon, Harry returned from the toilet with an indignant frown on his face.

"There's a big buck nigger prowling about outside," he said.

I looked up from my book. "Mmn?"

"A buck nigger. Walking about on the drive!" said Harry. His voice had lost its undead, born again calm, and sounded more like his old voice. The one I remembered arguing with.

I gave him a level, uncomprehending stare. I thought perhaps he was using some equestrian term, in the esoteric language of the horse world, to describe a deer, which sometimes flitted across the paddocks in graceful arching bounds before returning to the safety of End Wood. Then I noticed his expression and realised that he was talking about a person.

"What did you just say?" I cried, appalled.

"There's a nigger in the driveway," Harry croaked. "Go and see what he wants, Fy. Tell him this is private property."

"Perhaps he's got a horse he wants you to look after," I said.

Harry stared at me. He delivered one of his famous, twisted sneers, his mouth forming a supine S shape as he did so, and waved a dismissive hand towards me.

"Don't be ridiculous," he said.

"What's ridiculous?"

"Niggers never have any money," said Harry. "Take it from me, Fy, he's up to no good. Go and sort him out."

I looked at my father, and turned over Hélène's theory once again. Could she be right? Was the born again thing nothing more than a sham? Certainly, this was vintage Harry, and seemed to have no place in his new religion. But then I remembered the Mormons – who believed that black people were black with sin and would become white if they came to Jesus – and I was not so sure.

"He's not a nigger, dad, he's a black person," I said in a tired voice, pushing past him to the door. "I'll go and see what he wants. And if, for any reason, he *does* happen to want to leave a horse here, I'll just tell him to sod off, shall I?"

Harry whirled round as I stormed towards the front door, and opened his mouth to speak, but all that came out was a small, dry cough.

When I rounded the side of the house I saw Chris, my friend and fellow actor, pacing about on the drive. He looked nervous, but managed a tight smile as I approached.

"Oh thank god it's you," he said. "I thought I'd come to the wrong place." He looked about him in wonder, with the same mixture of awe and displacement that I had seen spread across the face of every friend I'd ever invited home. "I mean, this place is massive," he added, and his high, light voice floated from his large body as if escaping the pressure of his lungs, before being carried off on the gentle breeze which stirred the cherry trees behind me.

I shrugged. "It's smaller than it looks," I assured him.

"No. I mean, it's fantastic. Look at those doors!"

Chris pointed to the pair of studded wooden doors which stood on either side of the archway, folded back like the wings of some terrible, warlike bird. They were olive green and stood fifteen feet high. I couldn't remember ever having seen them shut, and doubted if it was even possible now. They had warped, settled on their hinges. I'd tried to shift them once, as a child, but had failed. Now the task would be even more difficult.

"Welcome to H M Prison Ravencrag," I said. Then, "So what are you doing here? I mean, it's great to see you, but this isn't a social visit?"

Chris looked at me and a flash of anxiety stole across his face. "It's Callum," he said. "Is he here with you?"

I shook my head. "No."

Chris sighed, and ran a nervous hand through his neatly tended two inch baby dreads. "Thought not. Looks like he's done a runner, then."

"What?"

"No one's seen him for the past week. And nobody's heard from him either. He usually calls John, like, every day, but there's been no word. And John's tried him at home, but no dice." Chris gave a half smile. "To tell you the truth, it's a bit of a relief. No offense, man, but it kind of gets on my tits. I mean, he's always asking for, like, money."

"And you never get it back?"

"Dead right."

"Me too," I laughed, and Chris relaxed.

"So, has he called you?" Chris asked me.

"Last I heard, he was out with you two, celebrating his

competition," I told him.

Chris's face darkened. "Oh yeah. That. And you've heard nothing since?"

"No."

"That's what I told John, but he insisted on checking with you anyway," Chris said.

"Presumably, he's been turning up for work?"

"Uh-uh. Hasn't even rung in sick. John checked. We'd have thought nothing of it, really, but he was just so *down* after he spoke to you that night. And then there was this, like, massive silence. Can only make you wonder." Chris grimaced. "But John says not to worry. Seems like he's pulled this sort of stunt before, back when they were at school together." Chris punched my arm, a gesture of solidarity and optimism. "I reckon you've got yourself one messed up boy there."

"Mmn," I said, sobered by this news. "By the way, how did you get here?" I could see no vehicle in the vicinity.

"I took the train to Norwich, and then I got a bus," said Chris. "It took fucking ages. And then I had to walk through the estate, and that drive is, like, *long*." He pointed back up the way he had come.

"But how did you find me?" I asked.

"Answer machine," Chris told me.

"I didn't leave the address on the message."

"No, and you didn't leave the number either, or I could have phoned instead," Chris said pointedly. "And that white trash operator would *not* divulge it, even though I said it was an emergency. But you did leave the name of the house, though." He adopted a hunched, pseudo-Gothic B Movie posture, and moaned "Ravencrag" in a creaky voice. "I mean, it's on the *map*, man!" He laughed and straightened up again.

I was impressed by his detective work. "Well now that

you're here, you might as well take a look around," I said.

"Can I meet your mad father?" Chris's dark eyes were aglitter with the possibility.

"I don't think that's a good idea."

"You mean he's not cool about visitors?"

"No. I mean he's not cool about meeting 'buck niggers'."

Chris's face hardened, his jaw set at a warlike angle. "I see your point, man. That would not be a good idea. I don't think he'd survive the encounter."

I looked at Chris, who seemed weirdly vulnerable despite his large physical bulk and handsome hard-boy face, and remembered that I used to envy him. It was much easier for a good black actor to get work than a good white one. But the tedium of dealing with racial intolerance he could keep.

I showed him the yard and the paddocks, but all the while Chris was distracted by the grandeur of his surroundings, and kept looking back at the imposing crenellations of the house. When the tour was over, we leant on a wooden fence embossed with constellations of green and golden litchens, and stared at a group of non descript horses.

"How much did it cost you to get here?" I said. Chris was out of work too, and as poor as I was. Poorer.

"About fifty quid. Why?"

"Okay. Wait here," I told him, and turned back towards the house.

Harry shuffled up to me as soon as I stepped into the hallway. "What did he want?" he demanded.

"Money," I replied.

"Humph! I told you so."

"I'm lending it to him," I added as I moved past him to collect my wallet from the telephone table. The remark was calculated to annoy, and succeeded.

"You fool. You'll never get it back."

I didn't want it back, it was a gift, but I wasn't going to tell Harry that. "Of course I will. He's a friend of mine from London," I said.

"How much did he want?"

"Fifty pounds," I told him.

"Fifty pounds! You're lending him fifty pounds?"

I straightened up and looked at my father, who seemed more agitated than the situation demanded. He was almost shaking with rage, his face gathered at the mouth, as if on a draw-string.

"Charity, dad. It's charity. Don't you believe in that? Besides, fifty pounds is nothing. Most of your horses cost thousands."

Harry, unable to argue with that, walked away, returning to the warmth of the sitting room. Once he'd left, I scooped up not my wallet, but his, from the table beside me. We'd already agreed that I should use his cash card for the household bills, once I'd got over my embarrassment about discussing money, and I felt that one added expense was justified. I was exacting this penalty for his rudeness and disapproval. I decided that his born again intolerance should cost him fifty pounds. Smiling, I left the house.

I drove Chris back to Norwich, where I withdrew five crisp ten pound notes from an ATM with my father's card.

"Thanks man," Chris said when I handed them over. He was both touched and relieved.

We had a coffee at the station whilst we waited for Chris's train back to London, and plotted our revenge against a world insensitive to our talent. When the train was announced, Chris stood and kissed me on both cheeks.

"Thanks again for the reimbursement," he said.

"Don't be ridiculous. It's the least I can do. Thanks for telling me about Callum."

"Man, it's nothing," Chris grinned, revealing his full complement of perfect teeth. "I'm your blood-brother, remember?" And we both laughed, recalling the ludicrous situation of playing twins separated at birth for our final show at drama school – the show in which Daniel Day Lewis had, for once, been relegated to a minor role.

When I got home, my father looked at me with suspicious eyes. "Has he gone now?" he said.

"Yes."

"Oh." Harry gave a definitive Prussian nod. "By the way, your agent rang while you were out. I said you'd call him back."

My heart beat faster, as it always did on such occasions. The prospect of an audition, of work, made me begin to tremble, as if I'd drunk three cups of strong coffee. It was the actor's disease at work in my veins again. My pathological optimism.

"Did he say what it was about?"

"No. But he knew who I was. He knew my name. How did he know that?"

"Because I've told him about you," I said.

Harry gave me another suspicious look. "He sounds Jewish," he said.

"Really? I'll tell him that," I laughed. "Perhaps it'll be good for business."

I went into the hall and dialled my agent's number from memory. It was the one number I never forgot.

"Hello Jim," I said when he picked up the phone, "it's Pip Winter here. I had a message to call you."

"Ah, Pip," my agent said. "Thanks for getting back to me." There was the sound of papers being rearranged on a desk, like the faint whispering of fire. "Yes, look, do you remember that audition you did last month for a new police series? *Rat Trap*?"

"Two auditions," I said with feeling. "They recalled me."

"Right. Well, they've been a long time sorting themselves out with it, but it seems they want to see you again."

"What, now? After all this time?" I cried. "I'd given up on that completely."

"I know. What can I say? These telly producers think we're all waiting to respond to their slightest whim." My agent laughed, a sound like a poorly tuned lawn mower engine. "So you're still interested?" he said.

I was annoyed that they had the nerve to ask to see me again. I'd read for a small bit part. Usually these minor parts were cast from a single reading, or, more often, from no reading at all – which explained why so much tv acting was atrocious. That was why I had been so surprised to be called back the first time. But to be asked to read for it *again* was stretching the point.

"I don't know," I said, hedging. "What do you think?"

"Well, it's a good part, Pip, and a year's contract," my agent told me. "You're up for one of the detectives, aren't you?"

"One of the regular characters?" My voice squeaked in surprise.

"Yes, I think so." More papers rustled on my agent's desk. "Yes, Detective Spencer, it says on the fax. Why? What did they see you for last time?"

"Some shop keeper, as I recall, who gets ripped off in episode one."

"Oh. Well, you've been promoted then."

"I see. In that case, I'm very interested," I laughed. "But I still can't believe they've taken so long to get back."

"Tell me about it! So anyway, they want to see you next week some time. I've no firm dates at the moment, of course, but I'll let you know as soon as I do."

"Okay, but it might be difficult to get down at short notice," I said.

I glanced up at my father, who was staring out of the hall window into the garden, pretending not to listen to our conversation. He seemed well enough at the moment, but, however much he claimed to have received a holy redemption from God, I knew his health was in delicate balance. He was a man on a high wire, edging across the Niagara Falls, and the slightest breath of wind could send him hurtling to his death. I had no way of knowing how well he would be next week. I couldn't know if I would be able to leave him for half a day and go down to London.

"I might have to arrange something in advance," I said.

"I see." My agent's voice lost its bantering tone. "How is he, Pip?"

"All right, actually, at the moment," I told him.

"Good, good. Well, as I say, I'll get in touch again when I know more, but in the meantime, read some detective novels! And well done, Pip. Let's hope you can swing this one."

"Absolutely," I said, and put the phone down.

"What was all that about?" Harry wanted to know as soon as I replaced the receiver. "Good news?"

"Possibly. Potential good news at any rate," I said.

"What?"

"I've got an audition for a part in a television series next week," I told him. "The new flagship police series for the BBC."

Harry nodded to himself and stared out of the hall window.

"If I get it, it will mean a lot of exposure, and that often leads to other work," I told him.

"But you've been on television before," Harry deadpanned.

84

"Not playing a proper part," I said. "All I've ever done so far has been a cough and a spit. This is a real job, a main character. And a year's contract, too."

Even as I spoke, I was growing more and more excited. The actor's disease was attacking every receptor cell in my brain, bullying me into a condition of dangerous hope. Finally, here was the prospect of proper work.

"This is exactly the kind of work I want," I said, unable to control my wide smile. "It could be a real break."

"But it's just an audition. You haven't got the part yet," said Harry. His voice was as flat as the Norfolk countryside which surrounded us.

I moved to the window and stood beside him, looking out at the glowering yew tree framed against the darkened winter sky. We were exactly the same height, my father and I, so physically alike, yet so utterly different within. Why did he not exhibit even the slightest flicker of interest at my news? I stole a sideways look at Harry, whose frail hands clutched at the windowsill for support as he gazed out over his garden and into the fields beyond, and wondered what he might be thinking. Looking at him, I couldn't tell. He was as unreadable to me as Sanskrit, as opaque as wave-worn glass. I decided to test him.

"Isn't it exciting?" I said.

"Mmn," said Harry. Then he turned and shuffled back towards the sitting room, and I wasn't even certain that he had heard me.

I stood alone in the cool, dark corridor, feeling like unwanted flotsam, and watched my father's receding back. I deflated, my mood punctured by Harry's indifference, and all the enthusiasm whispered out of me like stale air escaping from a wrecked tyre. It was at moments such as these that I missed Kate most. My mother and I had connected on some deep level, we were alike in all the important ways. I knew just how she would have reacted to the news. She would have thrown her arms up high, in a wide arc, and clapped her hands to her head, her mouth open wide in excitement. Her eyes would be bright, like green flames, and she would release a loud, euphoric whoop into the air, pushing her dark hair away from her forehead with her hands as she did so. She would express her excitement with her voice, her body, and her hands. She would run to me, and enfold me in her arms, planting a hot kiss on my temple as she did so. And she would tell me that she was proud of me.

All at once, I felt the bitter sting of tears pressing at my eyes, and blinked them away. That future had been denied me by mad, multiplying cells which had eaten Kate alive, leaving me alone with my impenetrable father. And soon he, too, would die, but more nastily, more strangely than Kate could ever have imagined. The tears pressed through again, feeling like salt and acid, and this time they fell, trickling down my surprised cheek like slow rain. I had not cried for twelve years, not since Kate's shiny coffin had been swallowed into the earth that rainy December morning, and I did not know for whom it was that my tears were falling now. For Harry? For Kate? For myself, the guilty living? It was a question with no answer.

This strange, sombre mood, which had descended on me with all the speed of a final curtain, stayed with me for the remainder of the day, and nothing could shake it off. Further, it was fuelled by a growing unease about Callum. Once I had seen Harry to bed – again he was able to climb the stairs to his room unaided – I wandered the house in an anchorless, listless fugue, visiting each room in turn and standing there in silence, letting the history of the house wash over me like a restless tide. I ran my fingers over every picture, I drank the darkness, and I pressed my cheeks against the cold walls as if the house itself could tell me that profound truth which would illuminate everything.

And the house answered me, drew me on into its heart. I found myself mounting the stairs which spiralled up to my father's room, and climbed still further, up the tiny narrow staircase which led from the upstairs landing to the attic. As I climbed, the darkness grew in depth, and the smell of dust accumulated in my nostrils. At the top of these secret stairs, barely wide enough for my narrow frame, there was a trap door and I reached up and pushed at it. It yielded with little resistance, revealing the maw of the attic as it swung open. I crawled inside and fumbled to turn on the light, which I knew was on the wall to my left, and the little room was flooded with a thin yellow glaze as my fingers found the switch.

I looked about me as I crouched in the cramped, freezing roof space, and my breath steamed from my mouth in the cold air. The attic was empty, but for a pair of covered cardboard boxes which stood in the far corner, and for a moment I wondered what had brought me here, what I was expecting to find. Slowly, I eased my way over to the boxes on hands and knees, careful not to make any noise as I was now directly above my father's room and I did not want to disturb him. My hands were caked in ancient dust. Kneeling beside the boxes, I rubbed my palms together and it dispersed about me like spores.

The first box contained women's clothes, neatly folded – underwear, blouses, and thin summer dresses – with a worn pair of white open-toed sandals resting on the top. Peering down through the layers of clothes, as a geologist might study the geostrata of a cliff face, I knew that the clothes were Kate's. They were the kind of thing she'd worn, and I also thought I recognised one or two of the dresses. I pressed my hand against them with a kind of reverence, a believer touching a relic of the True Cross, and felt an ache of sadness.

I was puzzled to find these things up here. I thought Harry had kept nothing of Kate's. Hélène had gone over to Ravencrag shortly after Kate died, and ruthlessly weeded everything from the house which might cause Harry pain – her reading glasses, her binoculars and star maps, her clothes, her shoes, and the prosthetic breast she wore after her mastectomy – leaving nothing but her sketch books, and various family photographs from which she smiled out at us, looking well and happy. So why had he kept these things? And if he *had* decided to keep them, then why were they hidden away up here, alone in the dark, where he would never see them?

I replaced the lid on the box and turned my attention to the second, which stood beside its neighbour like an identical twin. In here were Kate's sketch and watercolour books. I was even more surprised to find Kate's paintings up here, consigned to oblivion in the attic. Surely these were treasures, icons which Harry should want to enjoy? As ever, a veil fell over my eyes as I struggled to guess at my father's motives.

I lifted each sketch book out in turn, and studied every painting with a smile perched on my lips. They were tremendously comforting. My mother had painted them, her head bent low to the paper as she concentrated on the work, with the end of her pink tongue protruding from the corner of her mouth, and now I was looking at them with equal concentration, and I felt a real connection as my fingers caressed the paper. I had no talent for painting, so they delighted me with their vague definitions and subtlety of colour – all well-executed pastoral watercolours depicting wide open views with azure skies fading almost to white at the horizon. Kate must have painted them from memory of a time before her imprisonment in the centre of End Wood, or from her imagination, for not one of them was a view from Ravencrag. And I understood that completely. I had escaped on my bicycle, into school plays and amateur dramatics; Kate had escaped into her head, using a sable brush and paint.

I flipped the last sketch book closed on my knees and sighed, my head full of a golden nostalgia like the final days of summer. Replete, I leant back over the box to replace the books, and as I did so I noticed Kate's tape recorder lying there on the bottom. That last summer of her life, she had taken to carrying it around with her, to record observations, to make notes about what she might want to do to the garden, or to compose poetry as she sat on the weed-infested lawn which she'd given up tending.

"You think you're Barbara Cartland," I'd said, teasing her.

"Absolutely not," she'd replied. "I simply think it's time I dispensed with pens and paper. If I have a *thought*, I want to record it straight away. By the time I've found a pen and begun to write it down, I've often forgotten what it was. They're little devils like that – thoughts."

I picked up the tape recorder and noticed that there was a cassette still inside. With a ripple of fear, I wondered if there was anything on the tape, and pressed the play button without thinking how I might react to hearing my mother's voice from beyond the grave, but the batteries were dead and I heard nothing. Half relieved, but still curious, I removed the cassette and slipped it into my pocket, deciding to go back downstairs and play it on the machine in the sitting room. Nervous and excited, I quickly replaced all Kate's sketch books in the box, dropped the tape recorder on top of them, and made my way out of the attic, which had delivered me this most precious secret.

Once downstairs, I made myself a cup of coffee and returned to the sitting room, where I slipped the tape into the eager slot mouth of the machine. It was a unit capable of playing music in all formats, a present to Harry from Hélène, but it seemed barely used. There were no CDs in evidence and only a handful of cassettes. Harry's music collection consisted of about twenty vinyl albums, most of which I remembered from my childhood. I was surprised by this, because music was one of my great pleasures, but I supposed that Harry was not of a generation weaned on such things. Listening to music was not something he thought of doing very often.

I settled into the armchair which I had claimed as my own over the last fortnight, and the tape began. A foggy hissing resolved into a cough, and my throat clenched tight with emotion as I waited for my mother to speak to me. But it was not Kate's voice that I heard, wafting back through time like a smile. It was Harry's. And I sat like a petrified victim of Pompeii, unable to rise from my chair to turn off the machine, as the lava of Harry's words spewed into the room, cooled around me, and imprisoned me in a coffin of unrelenting stone.

"My name is Harry Winter," my father said in his new, chilling, featureless voice, "and this is my testimony before the One True God. I belong to the True Church and follow the True Faith. All other creeds are abomination, and the eyes of the Lord weep tears of vengeful sorrow when he hears them spoken. I have been baptized and Born Again. I am saved from the fires of Hell and I shall live forever in the Kingdom of the Righteous. Praise! Praise!

"I testify that my past life was a life of sin, a life of waste, a life of futility. It meant nothing, and was leading me to

Satan. But God has come to me and saved me from myself. He has given me Rock Hudson's disease, the scourge of Fy and his kind, and I have seen the light. I welcome his plague as I welcome Jesus."

There was a pause, and Harry coughed a thin, wheezy cough.

"When they told me I had... Aids... at the hospital, I was afraid, and I was angry. As proof of my old heathen self, I was frightened of dying, and angry that it was happening to me. I couldn't understand it. I couldn't believe it. But as I was leaving the hospital, a man came up to me. He was dressed in a black suit. He said, 'Brother, I can see from your face that you are troubled.' His face was quiet and grave. I said, 'It's worse than that, sport. I'm dying.' And he gave me a long look before saying, 'What is it?' I told him I had this Aids, and he took a step away from me, and looked at me again. 'Do you believe in the Lord?' he asked me. 'Do you believe in Jesus Christ our Saviour?' 'No,' I said, and I started to walk away. But he came after me, ran in front of me and stood in my path. 'But Jesus can save you,' he said. 'I doubt it,' I told him. 'I'm dying, and there's nothing he can do about that.' The man looked into my eyes. He was tall, and he looked down at me as I stared up at him. 'Oh, but He can! He can!' he said. 'Don't you see, this illness is a manifestation of your sin? Nothing more. If you repent your sins, have faith, and come to Jesus, you will be cured.' I was angry now. 'You mean, He'll cure me?' I snarled. 'No, no,' the man said. 'You will cure yourself! Your illness is your sin. Repent your sin and it will be gone.' I told him to leave me alone.

"When I got home, I took the pills the doctors gave me and I wandered around in shock. I was still reeling from the news of my health, and that man in the suit had disturbed me. For days, I didn't eat and I didn't sleep. I didn't even appreciate that I could breathe through my nose again. I kept on thinking that I had that actor's disease, and I was going to die. I didn't know what to do. How long I was like this, in the wilderness, I can't say. Maybe a week.

"I tried to keep my end up with the horses, doing the regular chores with Arthur, but the magic had gone. What was the point? And I was weak from lack of sleep. I was exhausted. Arthur kept asking me what was the matter, but I couldn't tell him. I wanted to, but I couldn't. And all the while that man in the black suit kept coming back into my mind. I imagined I saw him in the open doorways of stables, or walking across the paddocks, always smiling. So I stopped going outside. I went into the house and tried to shut him out. Arthur came to see me and I told him I had the flu, but he didn't believe me. So I told him I had cancer. He believed that.

"And then I had my vision. I was standing in the hall, looking up at the yew tree, and a white bird flew down and perched in the branches. As I looked, it grew larger and larger, its wings spreading out behind it, until I saw that it was an angel. He raised his arm and pointed at me, and I knew he wanted me to eat my pills, so I took them from my pocket and ate them, one by one. The angel smiled and told me to go to sleep now. He told me that he'd tell me secrets while I slept, secrets that God wanted me to hear.

"I fell to the ground and I shook all over. There was a bright, white light all around me, and a glow, like a smile in my heart that got bigger and bigger, warmer and warmer. My eyes were shut, but they seemed open, and I saw Jesus in front of me with his arms outstretched, welcoming me. He was speaking in a language that I had never heard, but I understood him and I answered in the same language. He knelt beside me and laid his hands on my head, and they felt warm and soft. Then there was a flash and I fell asleep.

"When I woke up, I knew that Jesus was alive inside me. I felt different, like a husk filled with light. Arthur was beside me, looking worried, but I told him I was well, that I had seen Jesus. 'And here is His first miracle,' I said. Because I saw that I was holding a card in my hands. It said: Rev. M. R. Johnson, Slyfold, with a phone number underneath. Arthur was sceptical. He is an Unbeliever.

"Once Arthur had gone, I phoned the Reverend, and as soon as he spoke I knew he was the man from the hospital. I told him my story and he seemed pleased, but not surprised. 'We must talk,' he said. He came out to see me at Ravencrag that evening, and we spoke about Jesus, about how he was living inside me, and about how I had been saved. It all made sense. He invited me to his church in Slyfold, and I went the next evening. And what praising there was! The power of Jesus was there in that church, touching each one of us. There was Healing. There was prayer. I felt my arms lifted above my head, I felt fire in my limbs, and again I fell to the floor and I spoke in Tongues. I prophesied Redemption, the absolution of sins, for all those reborn to Jesus.

"After the service, I spoke with the Reverend again, and he said I was ready to be Born. He said, 'If you live with Jesus in your heart, your sins will dissolve and your body will be whole.' 'Praise! I know it!' I said. And that night he, and three High Elders of the Church took me to the River Wensum, where I was stripped naked and baptized. The water was cold and it cleansed me. We are born naked and without sin, and I came out of the river Born Again and free of sin, naked like a child. They gave me a white robe to wear for the rest of that night.

"That is when my life began. I testify that my life before I came up out of the river was a life of sin, and it has been erased from the eyes of the Lord. When I was without Jesus my life was nothing, and only from the moment of my baptism has anything had true worth or meaning. My past life, and everything in it, was worthless and has been rejected. No love or bond has worth, but for the love of Jesus. This is the only love. And I know that this love will be rewarded. I shall be freed from my disease. Praise!"

The dead tape hissed on as I stared into the orange embers of the Norwegian stove, aghast. No wonder, then, that Harry had hidden those last reminders of Kate in the attic, I thought. They were the final chapter of his old life – the life of a thirty year marriage and two children – which he wanted to forget! I felt anger and resentment stir in my gut at the hubris of the notion, at the lack of regard for Kate, Hélène and myself. How could he shuck us off like that?

The dark stove held my eyes, its small cast-iron doors open wide, allowing the dense heat to spill into the room around me, and as I sat there, stunned, I studied the scene depicted in relief on the inside panel – a rustic scene of men chopping wood and carrying it back home on their shoulders, their bundles of sticks neatly lashed together with thick belts. The frisson I felt now was compounded by the knowledge that I had done exactly this once before. There was another night, twelve years ago, on which I had sat in this very chair, gazing into the Norwegian stove as if the force of my stare might have the power to change everything, and make my mother live.

The evening that Kate first felt the lump was like the start of a bad play, and it terrified us all. She looked up from her book, some endless family saga that she seemed to have been reading for months, and casually told us she could feel something the shape and size of a pear drop in her right breast.

"It feels like a bacon wart." she said.

Harry grunted, and I froze.

Rightly concerned, Kate went to Dr Daniels, the family doctor, the next day. He assured her it was benign – it was far too large, and had grown too fast, to be cancer. Nevertheless, he organised an appointment for her at the hospital at once, and we were unnerved by the speed with which it was all arranged. But at least he had said it was benign, we reminded ourselves, and we clung to those words like drowning men clutching at a lifeboat.

A week later, Kate went in for a biopsy of the breast lump. We were all tense and violently happy, awaiting the expected all-clear that the GP had intimated. Only Kate seemed controlled and calm.

"I'll be fine," she kept on saying. "Actually, I'm quite looking forward to it. Someone can look after me for a change."

To mask my nerves, I went into Norwich that afternoon and watched the special edition of Close Encounters twice through. I didn't want to go back home, I didn't want to hear anything bad. But I didn't stay out for long enough. When I returned, Harry had still not phoned in to find out what had happened, and when he could collect her from the hospital.

At the appointed time, Harry sat at the telephone table in the hall, like a nervous schoolboy, and called the hospital whilst Hélène and I crowded around him, casting worried looks at one another. We could only hear Harry's side of the conversation, of course, but what we heard turned our hearts to rock.

"Hello. I'm ringing about Mrs Winter... In Ward Six. How is she?... Oh good. And what...? I see... Did she have the major operation?" Harry's voice, and face, dropped. "I see... Yes, thank you. I'll come in and see her tomorrow... Yes, thank you. Goodbye."

Harry rose from the table like an old man, and looked over our heads, at a point on the wall behind us.

"It was cancer," he said simply, tossing the word out like a piece of trivia. "She had to have a mastectomy. But it went very well and they've got it all out. They think she'll be fine." And with that, he left the room like a famous actor exiting a film set, leaving the wreckage behind him.

My sister and I sat in the sitting room for hours, drinking tea and staring into space. We didn't know what to do, and sat quietly together, mute and numb, exchanging miserable looks. Above our heads we could hear dull bangs and thuds, as if Harry was rearranging the bedroom furniture.

"Jesus, Pip," Hélène said into the silence, "will you be all right here? On your own?"

"I'm not on my own," I replied, and cast my eyes upwards.

"I think you are," she said.

Kate came out of hospital a week later. For a while, we treated her like a fragile china doll, or a rare, exotic plant, but in time we relaxed and life returned to normal. She began a course of radiotherapy – the belt and braces approach, as her surgeon called it – and she responded well. They called her a wonder patient. And they told us everything was going to be all right.

That autumn, I was offered a place at drama school in Bristol. It seemed that this was as much a filip to Kate as it was to me, and gradually, as I saw her return to health with steady determination, the tourniquet of fear, which had wrapped itself around my heart, loosened.

Over the next four years we became experts on breast cancer. We found out that if Kate presented no further cancers within five years, her prognosis was good; if she went ten years, then she was 'cured'. They were tense years, but the tension was locked away in secret parts of each one of us, invisible to all but ourselves, and examined in private. All the time we were counting off the months, counting off the years, willing her to *exceed five, and then ten, willing her to beat the disease. During those years, it was as if the whole family was holding its breath, and the effort was palpable. Our incredible, robust mother could not possibly die. It was impossible. We were not ready.*

It seemed that my sister was more traumatized by Kate's mastectomy than by the conquered cancer and its threat to her life, but Kate, as ever, took it in her stride and treated it as something of a joke. She experimented with foam, balled-up socks, and plastic pseudo-breasts before finally settling for a gel-filled, purpose built prosthesis – pink and squashy, like a stress ball – which she named George. But she did not always bother to wear it. Hélène, who no longer lived at home, was horrified and embarrassed whenever she found Kate breastless, whereas I was used to finding George nestling amongst the apples and bananas in the fruit bowl on the dining table, like some exotic, genetically engineered fruit.

"Only having one breast is nothing to be ashamed of," Kate told me once as we sat in the garden, sunbathing. She was not wearing George that day and was lying in a lawn chair a few feet from me, half flat-chested. "If it was good enough for the Amazons, then it's good enough for me," she said, pushing her hair away from her face with both hands.

"Does it feel odd?" I asked her.

"Not really. Physically, it's a bit strange, I suppose. Sometimes I lose my balance when I'm star-gazing. But I don't feel any less of a woman, if that's what you mean."

"Is that what people feel?"

"Quite often, apparently. That's what they told me at the hospital. But I never did, probably because I'm the age I am. I expect it would be different for Hélène."

Kate paused to apply sun cream to her forearms, rubbing with swift circular motions. She proffered the plastic bottle to me, but I waved it away.

"Lots of men, I mean the husbands, find it difficult, too," Kate

said, floating the words into the syrupy afternoon. "Some relationships get rocky because of it. The men don't fancy their wives any more..."

I looked across at my mother, but her eyes were closed and I could not tell what it was that she was trying to tell me, if anything. Kate often talked to me like this. We had conversations that I knew she did not have with my sister, or Harry, and I wondered what it was that made her feel able to say these things to me. Was it because I was gay? Did this, somehow, place me in a special category all of my own? I thought of Harry, and wondered if he had ceased to find my mother attractive for the loss of a few pounds of flesh.

It was not until months later that the watching began. I did it secretly during the Christmas break in my final year at drama school. I didn't tell anyone because I didn't want to alarm my sister, and I was unable to discuss it with my unreachable father – who had receded still further into his regime of horses. But as I watched, I noticed that Kate began to slow down. It was almost imperceptible at first, but as I silently counted out the months since Kate's operation, the signs got larger and more numerous: She puffed whilst climbing the stairs, a staccato exhalation to accompany each step, with her lower lip extended beyond her upper one, as if blowing phantom strands of hair from her face; she grunted when she bent over to retrieve a pan from the cupboard below the sink; she walked slower, and less far, on our daily meanderings through End Wood as the dogs thundered at our heels; and she fell asleep whilst reading, something she had never done before.

And the following spring – as the daffodils pushed up beneath the kitchen window, and thin, pale green shoots reached for the sun in the garden beds – my mother began to die.

"There's something wrong," she told me one night as we stood together in the kitchen. "I know there is." Her eyes were shiny and wet. "There's something going on in here." She pressed her abdomen with her right hand to indicate what she meant.

I stared at her, rigid. My suspicions were confirmed. At once I dived into her arms and she hugged me like a bear. I was twenty-four years old, just graduated from drama school, and I had never needed a hug from my mother as badly as I did just then. Her flesh was warm and forgiving as I leant into her, and she rubbed my back with her hand as we rocked back and forth, comforting one another. Neither of us cried, our communication was deeper than that. We had a bond of complete, wordless, understanding.

"If it's the cancer again," Kate said, and I heard the infinitesimal hesitation in her voice before she uttered that dread word, "then we're going to have to be brave."

"I can't," I said.

"Yes, you can. You can," Kate whispered, her mouth close to my unwilling ear.

She hugged me closer still, and I felt something brittle inside me, like a rod of frozen iron. Better to be a reed, I thought, a reed that can bend. But I knew I was fragile as Venetian glass.

"It might be nothing, Pip," she whispered. "It might be nothing." But we both knew it wasn't.

She went into hospital again about a fortnight later, her face mild, giving nothing away. They were due to perform a laparotomy – something like a Caesarian section – and have a general inspection of the state of her insides, with a view to removing any offending tissue. That day was chilly for the time of year, and I spent the afternoon huddled up by the Norwegian stove, trying, and failing, to read a book.

Harry took Hélène to the hospital with him on the afternoon of Kate's operation. As I waved them off, all three of us wore quavering, unreal smiles because we knew that this was the last moment we'd ever feel like a whole family. Even Harry, imprisoned behind his wall of indifference, was part of it. It was the nearest I had ever come to feeling sorry for him.

By the time six o'clock came, and they had still not returned from the hospital, I knew the news would be bad. I began to feel desiccated inside. I sat in an armchair and stared fixedly into the Norwegian stove, feeling the heat on my young face, and told myself that Kate was going to die. I knew with awful certainty that this was the news they would bring, and I spoke the words aloud to myself, alone in the sitting room, to see if I could bear them. But the sounds I made seemed to have nothing to do with me as they fell from my lips into the silent room.

When my father and sister did return, porridge-grey and tired, they drifted into the room like aimless ghosts. Harry turned away from me and sat at his desk, round the corner of the L shaped room, saying nothing. Hélène sighed and shrugged her big shoulders.

"She was riddled with it, Pip," she told me. "When they opened her up, it was everywhere." Her voice was flat and devoid of expression, as were her eyes.

"What did they do?"

"Nothing. They just sewed her back up again. They say she's got a month to live, maybe two at the most."

"Oh."

That most insubstantial word encapsulated everything in my heart at that moment. Nothing further needed to be said. I felt strange, dislocated, and free of all emotion. Numbness, and shock, had claimed me. The room suddenly seemed unbearably quiet, but for the insistent ticking of Hélène's cuckoo clock.

"They've told her the operation was a success," Hélène said. "They've told her she's going to be fine."

With that, her voice faltered at last, she lost control of her lower jaw, and she ran from the room with a hand pressed over her mouth. My father and I did not move and said nothing. After a while Harry turned to look at me, and I looked away, directing my gaze towards the fire again. That was the moment when Harry might have said what he felt about Kate's diagnosis and his impending bereavement, but he didn't. Instead, he sat and stared at the wall whilst the new silence rolled around us like velvet, slowly stopping our mouths.

I was never sure, after that, who was playing the game. The game of pretending she wasn't going to die. Kate returned from the hospital bright and cheerful, as if she really did believe she was going to be fine, and Harry behaved as if nothing whatever had happened: He still insisted on watching the racing, even if Kate wanted to watch a black and white film on another channel; he still expected her to prepare all the meals; he still spent all his time out in the yard, or in the paddocks. My sister also took part in the game – I could see it in her tight, brave smile as she handed Kate an extra special gift on Mother's Day, and on her birthday, three weeks later. This was the way of my family. We, who talked so much yet said so little, would rather deny Kate's illness than confront and discuss it. All, that was, except me.

A month passed, then two, and soon Kate was living on borrowed time. She was having chemotherapy at that time, a vast cocktail of drugs which seemed to be helping. I would catch sight of Kate sometimes, sitting in the garden with her newly acquired tape recorder, and find myself wondering if she really was curing herself after all, like one of those miracle stories one reads of in colour supplements. Her face seemed radiant, healthy, happy – not the face of a dying person at all.

The third month after Kate's pretend operation, in this growing atmosphere of fragile optimism, I landed my first ever acting job. A series of lager commercials, in which I had to lip sync to sixties pop songs.

"But why are you doing adverts, Pip?" Kate asked me in her most derisive tone. "You're an actor. Richard would never think of doing one."

Uncle Richard was the one who had warned me not to take to the stage. He was an old fashioned actor, and thought adverts low and common.

"Commercials are considered chic these days," I told her.

"Besides, it's the only way you can make any money in this business."

"Will they make you rich and famous?"

"No," I laughed. "They'll make me temporarily well-off, and unknown."

I was trying to sound worldly and knowledgeable to cover the fact that I was green and inexperienced. If I had known at the time how true those words would be, perhaps I might have tried to cure myself, then and there, of the actor's disease, which even then coursed through my blood like hungry fire.

I was away filming the commercials for a fortnight, and when I returned, Kate had changed. She was pale, and had lost weight.

"It's these new pills," she told me as we sat in the sitting room on the afternoon of my return. "They make me feel so sick all the time. I'm fed up with it."

"Stop taking them, then."

"I can't do that!" My mother opened her eyes wide as windows.

"Why not?"

"You're not supposed to. I mean, aren't they helping?"

"Depends what you mean by helping. If they're making you feel ill, then they're not helping much, are they?"

"But aren't they keeping the cancer at bay?" She lowered her voice as she said this, as if Harry, or the cells themselves, might overhear.

I shrugged.

"You really think it would be all right to stop?"

"Of course," I told her, "if you want to."

With that she brightened considerably. "I'm so glad," she said, and rose from her chair and went upstairs.

She returned a couple of minutes later with two little brown bottles. In a party mood, she threw open the bathroom door, unscrewed the lid of the first bottle and poured its contents into the waiting toilet. Then she emptied the other. She remained still *for some moments, and stared down at her rejected medication, which lay shimmering beneath the silent water, with a satisfied expression.*

"I don't think we need to tell Harry about this, do we?" she said as she flushed the toilet and her pills began their slow journey to the sea. "It can be our secret."

I nodded, feeling perturbed. "Have you thrown all of them away?" I asked.

"Oh no," Kate replied, beaming me a hesitant smile, "just those awful new ones."

"Good," I said, relieved. "I approve."

There was a balanced moment, where we looked at each other without speaking. Kate came up to me, held me by the shoulders, and planted one of her famous kisses on my temple. Then she released me and stepped back.

"I love you, Pip," she said.

I smiled the thinnest of smiles, suddenly aware that all this time Kate had been playing another game. A game entirely of her own. Of course she had known that she was dying. She wasn't stupid.

Shortly after that, Kate's stomach began to fill up with fluid. After ten days, it had distended so much that she had to resort to wearing shapeless maternity smocks.

"I look pregnant," she shrieked. "A fifty-three year old pregnant woman! Ring up the Guinness Book of Records *at once!"*

I was alarmed at this sudden change, and felt certain that Kate was nearing the end of her borrowed time, but the doctors at the hospital thought otherwise. They stuck a tube into her abdomen, drained the fluid out, and she deflated like a spent balloon after a party. Then they sent her home. The operation took half an hour.

"And that's all there is to it," she explained, clearly relieved, on her return.

This pattern continued. She would slowly swell over a

period of time, until her stomach was tight as a drum, then she would visit the hospital to be drained, and return home to repeat the process. It went on for weeks, and seemed to be a relatively stable, if bizarre, condition.

I was not as concerned as I might have been, therefore, when I got my first proper theatre part and had to leave Kate alone at Ravencrag, in Harry's care. I'd been cast in a small-scale production of Great Expectations, *performed by five actors, touring round the country for a proposed six months. The work was exciting and tiring, and I reported back to Kate by phone on a regular basis. She wanted to know all about it.*

"But how are you?" I'd ask her, once she'd pumped me of all my news.

"The same as ever," she'd say. "Still going up and down."

She said this every time I phoned her, that she was 'still going up and down' – alluding, of course, to her miraculous stomach – until one evening, in early December, when her answer was different.

"They had a trainee draining me today," she said.

"What does that mean?"

"Oh, it's quite a simple thing to do, I suppose. They just push a tube into my stomach, and hey presto. But this time, with this trainee, it felt different."

My heart began to bang in my chest, slamming about like a caged bird. "Different?" I said.

"Yes. Usually, I feel a sort of 'pop' as the needle goes through me, but this time I felt another one, deeper down. I think they punctured something."

"Did you tell them about it?" I cried.

"I didn't like to," Kate replied in a quiet voice. "He was only a trainee."

"How long ago was this?" I demanded, aware that I was sounding like my father, with his bullying questions, but unable to curb my anxiety.

"Two days."

"And how are you now?"

"Fine. Just... feeling thicker in the middle."

"Does dad know?"

"Goodness, no," Kate said, her voice airy. "What would I tell him that for? You know him, he'd be wanting a bulletin update every ten minutes."

"But you're sure you're okay?"

"Yes. I'm sure."

I was very worried by this. All the next day I was unable to concentrate, and missed an important entrance during the show. It struck me, then, as it has countless times since, how ridiculous the popular notion of 'the show must go on' really is. I phoned home immediately after the performance, but it was Harry who answered, not Kate.

"How is she?" I said.

"Resting," Harry said.

"What's the matter with her?"

"She's tired, Fy."

"But what's wrong with her?"

"How should I know?" my father snapped.

"Do you think I should come home?" I said. This would be awkward and difficult, but not impossible. "I could get a train right now."

"No!" my father cried, his voice forceful. "Don't do that, you might worry her. She's not on her deathbed, Fy. She'll probably bounce back. You know her."

I so wanted to believe him that I pushed away what Kate had told me the previous evening. "You're sure I shouldn't come back?" I asked him.

"Yes, quite sure," my father said.

There followed a terrible three days in which I found it impossible to reach a telephone. Our venues – strange village halls and other non-theatre buildings – seemed bereft of all modern appliances, as did the ramshackle holiday cottage in which we were currently staying, situated on a remote hillside in Shropshire. On the third night, eaten with anxiety, I drove the company van through miles of winding lanes in search of a public phone still in working order. Eventually I found one.

"Hello Pip," came a thin voice at the other end. "Thank god you've called."

For a moment I thought it was Kate, but then I realised it was Hélène. "What are you doing at Ravencrag?" I said. "Where's Harry? Where's Kate?"

"Don't ask, Pip. Just come home. You've got to come home."

A cold sweat broke out all over me as I huddled in my phone booth. I knew what this meant. "When?" I rasped.

"Now, Pip. Come now." Her tired, miserable voice cut through me like a rusty saw.

"What's going on?"

"Dad's out at the pub. I'm here with her. But she doesn't know who I am. And she looks so... Just come home." The last word extruded into a painful sob which made a lump appear in my own throat.

"I'm coming, 'Lène," I whispered, unable to swallow. "I'm coming."

In fact, there were no trains out of Iron Bridge at this time, so I knew I'd have to wait until morning, but Hélène needed to know I was coming, she needed to feel she wasn't alone. I drove back to our digs, packed my bags, and told the stage manager I was leaving in the morning.

"You can't do that," he said.

"Watch me," I replied, my eyes steely. "It's only five days until the Christmas break anyway. You can muddle through 'til then."

"Mike will go ballistic."

"So what's he going to do? Sue me?"

"He might."

"I'll live with it," I said, and headed for my bedroom. But I did not sleep.

The next day my fellow actors, somewhat more laid back than the stage manager, drove me to the station.

"See you after Christmas," they chorused in low voices.

"Thanks. Take care."

And so I began my slow, convoluted cross-country journey from Wales to East Anglia, but by the time I arrived at Ravencrag I was too late. Kate had died earlier that night, the night of December 18th.

The days following Kate's death were bitter. A raw Norfolk wind blew up from the North Sea, and managed to wheedle through every window and door of our drafty house. In every room a low, keening moan could be heard, as if the house itself was howling at our loss. I couldn't bear it, and to escape the ghostly wail I took long, numbing walks around End Wood, but even here the trees groaned and squeaked above my head, protesting at the gale. It seemed the whole world was the sound board for the shrieking of my silent heart. I felt leaden during those terrible days, permanently tired yet unable to sleep.

Hélène remained at Ravencrag, and soon we were joined by two distant aunts of whom I had only the barest recollection, and we sat about for days and days in nervous, brittle humour, whilst Harry anaesthetized himself at the Shepherd & Dog. We hardly saw him, but I heard him return home each night, staggering upstairs to his half-empty bed.

The tension mounted as the days passed. Because of the time of year – oh, Happy Christmas! – Kate's funeral could not be scheduled immediately. We would have to wait until the festivities were over, so were consigned to a ten day state of limbo, during which we all felt suspended from life. Because we knew that we were waiting, it was impossible to act normally, however hard we tried.

One afternoon Hélène and I drove into Norwich, in a vain

attempt to lift our spirits with some post-Christmas shopping, but I couldn't connect. As people drifted past me in the hushed precinct, I wondered how they could smile and laugh when I had sustained this killing blow. I felt that it must be obvious, and that they should respect my sadness. I resented their cheerfulness, and I resented the bright decorations in all the shop windows. I wanted to run inside and tear them all down, screaming, 'Don't you realise my mother has died?'

"I hate this," I told Hélène as we slow-marched our way past a shoe shop displaying vacuous, happy Santas and red-nosed reindeer.

She looked at me for a moment. "Me too," she said, clearly relieved. "Let's go home."

At night I entertained strange, morbid thoughts. I imagined Kate lying in a steel drawer at the morgue, and could not get the picture out of my mind. I wondered who she was lying next to, and I wondered what expression her face wore. These thoughts, which wound round my brain like writhing worms, served only to make sleep impossible. I hated the idea of her lying in state in a glorified refrigerator. I wanted her gone, buried, finished. I wanted the circle to be closed. Then, perhaps, I could begin to grieve. All this waiting was unseemly.

Finally, the grim day dawned, four days after Christmas, and although I felt as if I had been awake all night, I must have slept because I awoke that morning with a terrible sense of fear. I was terrified of my emotions. As yet, my sadness had not expressed itself in any outward form, but I knew the dam of my resilience was set to crumble, and didn't know where it would stop. I looked out of the window as I dressed, and somehow it seemed entirely fitting that a thick, slow rain was falling.

We were all quiet and sombre that morning, steeling ourselves for the day ahead, and sat about like cataplectics. All, that is, except Harry, who wandered through the house with the false jollity of an air steward. He behaved as if he were going to a

108

party, rather than the funeral of his wife of thirty years, and it made me furious.

Finally, after two hours of purgatory – during which Harry prattled on about some horse that he'd just pin-fired – I could stand it no longer. I jumped up, threw on an old overcoat and left the house, heading for the tool shed, which stood in the corner of the garden. With no clear idea of what I was doing, except some vague notion of expiating the shapeless fury which billowed inside me like a thunderstorm, I grabbed a heavy Spear & Jackson axe, slung it over my shoulder, then made off over Primrose paddock towards End Wood beneath a curtain of dull rain.

I walked fast, with my head down, and by the time I reached the wood I was breathing heavily. I was soaked through, with my hair flopping into my eyes, but I didn't care. I plunged deeper into the wood and walked on, stumbling through the slick, muddy paths until I reached the gallop where Harry had schooled Hélène and me as we thundered up and down, perfecting our technique and learning our balance. There before me stood the practice brush fences that I had jumped so many times, and as I stared at them, through the gloom, I realised that a part of me had always known that I would end up here.

I leapt over the barbed-wire cordon which separated the wood from the gallop, and strode over to the nearer of the fences, where I raised my axe and attacked the left-hand stanchion with all the fervour of a psychopath. I chopped and chopped, emitting atavistic grunts of effort, until it splintered in half and sagged to the ground, then I moved on and gave similar treatment to the other fence. Afterwards, feeling hot, breathless and strangely righteous I straightened up and made back towards the house, but by the time I got there, I could no longer remember why I had destroyed the fences. As soon as I got in, I went upstairs and had a long, hot bath. Nobody asked me what I had been doing outside in the rain.

The funeral was set for two o clock, in the grey flint church in

Bruxley, where we'd attended that midnight carol service all those years before. Two estate cars had been arranged to take us there, but by half past one, mysteriously, only one had arrived. Harry and the aunts went off in it, along with their husbands, who had turned up the previous evening. Theoretically, Hélène and I could have squeezed inside as well, but it was a long drive to Bruxley, and somehow it did not seem fitting. Also, we thought the other car may yet appear, so we elected to stay behind for a few minutes, and follow on in Hélène's own car if it did not arrive.

Five minutes later, however, the second limousine did indeed pull up, and we jumped in, now anxious about the time. I felt like a charlatan dignitary as I slumped on the vast upholstered back seat. The sedate journey seemed desperately slow.

As I had feared, we were late, the very last to arrive, and when we reached the church doors, which seemed to be smudged black in the pouring rain, everyone turned to look at us. I was surprised, and gratified, by how many people had turned out, but their numbers daunted me as we proceeded up the aisle to take our place in the front pew – the pew reserved for the next of kin – followed by rows of sympathetic, curious eyes. We were the only source of noise in that still, hushed hall. As we walked up the aisle, with all those heads turning as we went past, Hélène held on to my hand so hard that I thought the bones might crack. But I didn't mind. The pain was a welcome distraction from the clamour in my heart, the itching in my eyes, and my sudden inability to swallow. Because it was only then that the full horror of it hit me – that my mother was dead, and I had missed her by a day. By the time we took our places in the pew, Hélène's shoulders were shaking, her cheeks wet with tears. But I had been struck dumb.

Throughout the service, I couldn't take my eyes off the coffin, which lay barely five feet from where I sat, and was flanked by two large vases of chrysanthemums, Kate's favourite flowers. The

coffin seemed absurdly small. How could this lacquered box —
gleaming like some miraculous, exotic nut, and barely bigger
than a cradle — house the hugeness that was my mother? It was
impossible. That was the thought which turned in my head as the
rituals of kneeling, singing, and praying took place around me.

So it was not until later, as I saw her lowered into the ground,
oblivious to the wind and rain which beat about us, and heard the
heavy clods of Norfolk mud boom gently over her forever quiet,
upturned face, that I began, at last, to cry. My sobs were dry,
guttural, and painful, forcing themselves up from the deepest
reaches of my heart, and sounded almost inhuman to my ear.
Slowly, with aching throat, I raised my hot eyes from her grave to
seek solace in the seamless ceiling of cloud, but the tears kept
coming. And they were wetter than the rain.

A log popped in the Norwegian stove, and I jolted from
my reverie. The tape machine, which I had left running
when Harry's bizarre autobiography had finished, was
emitting a low whine as it strained against the wound tape,
and I rose from my chair and went to turn it off.

As I crossed the room, I was freshly astonished by my
father's excision of us all from his new life. All the love, all
the care, all the emotional energy which we'd poured into
Kate over the four years of her illness were, as far as he
was concerned, nothing. Bundling Kate's things into
cardboard boxes, to lie hidden in the attic, was his
statement that our heartache had been misplaced, that our
lives had been meaningless because they were without
God. According to his own gospel, the hugeness that was
Kate was rendered void. Evil, even. I had never despised
him more.

And from that moment, I was haunted by his callous
betrayal of our lives. I couldn't get it out of my head – that
anodyne, bleating voice recanting all but the most recent

past, as if God himself could be fooled. I slept badly for several nights, unable to rid myself of the thought, like an oyster stuck with an irritating grain of sand. But unlike that diligent creature I did not manufacture a pearl. Instead, I produced a dense nugget of disgust.

I found it impossible to stay in the house with Harry, and wandered through the grounds lost to a wordless anger, the wet Norfolk mists which cloaked me echoing the dull thoughts that whirled in my head: In my father's new streamlined, spiritually efficient world, I was an unwelcome reminder of his old, sinful life. I was the pebble in his shoe, his crown of thorns. With this realisation, I felt my presence at Ravencrag grow more tenuous, more difficult.

Nothing was ever said, of course. Instead, we retreated still further into our respective castles of silence – long, heavy silences more eloquent than any words could have been. Harry sensed my withdrawal but could not guess at the reasons, and to make up for it, he began to murmur prayers under his breath in a continuous stream. Whenever I glanced at him I saw his lips fluttering like slow moths, calling on his cruel, unforgiving god as the knuckles of his clasped hands grew white with tension.

In protest, I read my books with furious concentration, scarcely looking up, and performed my chores about the house as if every one of them was an act against my principles. I sullenly trudged to the wood shed to collect logs for the stove, I prepared dull, efficient meals, and I administered Harry's drugs with all the ambivalence of a junior doctor at the end of a forty-eight hour shift. But I didn't talk to him. I never asked him how he was. Why should I? I was nothing to him, so why should he be anything more to me? I was behaving like an adolescent, and I was enjoying it. It was easier like this. Anger was, at least, an emotion.

But I hadn't cut myself entirely loose from my father. A part of me was still curious about him. I knew that his current good health was temporary, as transient as the mist which hung over Ravencrag like ectoplasm, and I wondered what he would do when it failed at last. He believed that God had cured him. What would happen when he was faced with the unpalatable truth that he'd been subject to the ultimate placebo? To my chagrin, I was actually looking forward to the endgame, although I knew it could still be some way off. He did indeed seem surprisingly well, if tired. What had happened to the menace in his lungs? When would it strike again? I would have to wait.

Four difficult days later, my agent phoned, and mercifully broke the spell of my obsession. It was the early evening, about six, and I was in the middle of preparing a meal. An unusual time for him to call.

"Hello, Pip? It's Jim Johnson here."

"Hello," I said. "What's up?"

I tried to sound casual, but I was thrown off balance by him. I had not actually forgotten about my forthcoming casting, but my father's revelations, and the memories it had thrown up, had submerged it somewhat. It did not seem a very important part of my life just now.

"I've got news about this *Rat Trap* thing," my agent said in that easy voice of his, a voice that could wheedle contracts out of producers, but never for me. "They want to see you on Friday. Does that suit?"

I stared out of the hall window, at the thick, motionless mist which seemed to continually press against the panes.

"Friday's fine," I said in a dead voice. "What time?"

"I've told them you're coming in from the sticks," he said, "so we've got a provisional two-thirty here.

113

How's that?"

"Perfect. I hate early starts," I said.

"All right. I'll confirm that with them for you. And it's in the usual place. Union House in Shepherd's Bush."

"Thanks."

"You'll be able to get down all right? With your father..."

"Oh yes," I said. It was only two days away and Harry seemed stable. "That won't be a problem."

"Good. I'm glad to hear that, for both of you," my agent said. "And Pip? Wear a suit on Friday. Detective Spencer's a bit of a smoothie."

"So why are they interested in me?" I said. It still seemed as if I was discussing a third party. There was no feeling of reality about any of it.

"Don't be like that, Pip," my agent told me. "You may be short, but you *are* suave. Remember that on Friday."

This was my big problem. I saw myself one way but other people, casting people, saw me differently. I thought I was rough and rugged, if diminutive, whilst others viewed me as dapper and a little bit fey. I was like a four stone anorexic who is convinced that they are fat.

"I'll try," I promised him.

"Good," my agent said. "And call me afterwards. Tell me how it goes. I feel good about this one."

"Me too," I lied.

As I put the phone down my enthusiasm for the job suddenly returned, as if a switch had been thrown, and I smiled to myself. This was exactly what I needed – something to focus my attention for a day or two, outside the confines of Ravencrag and my unreadable father – and I patted myself on the back with my right hand, hooking my arm over my left shoulder, to congratulate myself. It was a trick I'd copied from Martina Navratilova.

The phone had been back in its cradle for less than ten

seconds when it rang again, and I snatched up the receiver at once. I had not even had time to rise from the telephone table.

"What did you forget to tell me?" I laughed.

"What?" It was Hélène's voice.

"Sorry 'Lène. I thought you were my agent."

"Oh," she said. "Listen, I thought I'd come up and see you. I've threatened to come often enough. Is now a good time?"

"Now?" I was surprised. Hélène was usually more organised than this, less spontaneous.

"Yes. My briefing didn't take nearly as long as I thought it would, so I've got hours to kill. Ewan's not expecting me back until late."

"Okay then. Great," I said, pleased. Her visit would be a relief from the sapping monotony of my lonely vigil. "When can I expect you?"

"Ninety minutes? I'll set off immediately," she said.

Half an hour after I'd perfunctorily fed Harry his pills, and overseen his ascent up the staircase, she arrived on the doorstep. I hardly recognised her. Her skin seemed thin and pale, her eyes were dark and sunken with fatigue, and her hair hung limp from her head like a cheap wig.

"I know. I look dreadful," she said as I studied her on the threshold, and she tossed me the ghost of a smile. "This is the post-courtroom me."

"I'm not much competition myself," I said, referring to my own sallow complexion due to lack of sleep.

Hélène stooped down to my level and we swapped brief sibling kisses, then I ushered her into the gloomy kitchen, which was suffused with winter cold. At once, she sat down at the small formica work table in the corner, a relic of our vanished childhood, and rummaged in her bag for cigarettes whilst I busied myself with the ritual of tea.

"Do you want one?" she said, retrieving a packet from within.

I shook my head. "I don't smoke real cigarettes," I said.

Hélène arched her eyebrows as she held the cigarette, unlit, between her lips. "I take it that this one can be transformed?"

"Absolutely," I said.

"You're on," said Hélène with a grin. She then proceeded to pick at the cigarette with her nails, in order to free the tobacco within.

I was feeling in great need of a lift myself, and willingly trotted upstairs to fetch my little red box. When I returned, Hélène was sitting at the table surrounded by numerous gutted cigarettes and several strange origami structures which I guessed must be reject joints.

"I've lost the knack of this," she smiled as I sat down beside her. "Maybe you should do it."

She handed me a twisted knot of paper.

"You have to use Rizla papers, not the cigarette paper," I told her as I regarded her latest failed spliff. "They don't have any glue on them."

"Oh yes, of course!" she nodded, and grabbed the papers from my outstretched hand. Then she set about making a new joint. "It's all coming back to me now," Hélène cried as she sprinkled tobacco on a promising-looking field of Rizla paper. "I feel positively adolescent."

I handed her the dope, which she warmed and crumbled.

"Steady on," I cried in alarm. "That's strong stuff."

"Ha!" said Hélène, waving a dismissive hand in my direction. "It's mostly placebo effect, if you ask me. It would take a lot more than that to get *me* stoned."

She may have been right, speaking for herself, but I knew that I would be totally blown. Perhaps it wasn't such a good idea. Then I thought of Harry's betrayal, of the still-missing Callum, and my forthcoming audition, and took a long drag on the joint.

Twenty minutes later we were nodding quietly to ourselves, smiling little space cadet smiles at one another.

"My eyeballs have gone dry, and I feel as if a gerbil just died in my mouth," Hélène complained.

"Brilliant," I said, "the dope's working."

We both found this unbelievably funny.

"God. This always reminds me of college," I said.

"You didn't go to college."

"Drama school, then."

We giggled some more, then lapsed into a companionable silence.

"Did you have to balance books on your head?"

"What?"

"At drama school. I thought you had to walk about with book on your head."

"What would I do that for?"

"I don't know. Deportment."

"No, I never did that. But I did have to wear a skirt," I said. "Not all the time, of course. Just for some of the movement classes."

"Why?"

"Can't remember."

"That's weird, Pip."

"Hmm."

I looked around the kitchen, which had now become extremely beautiful, and fetched a glass of water to rinse my gummy mouth. It tasted soft, slippery and strange to my southern palate. I was used to the hard chalky water of the Thames valley.

"So what *did* you learn at drama school?"

I looked over to Hélène, who was tracing round the

edge of the table with her fingers, her face expressing the rapt concentration of a five year old, and considered her question carefully for some moments. It was something I'd asked myself many times.

"I learned to perform fellatio to a professional standard," I said, and smiled as I remembered Clive, my enthusiastic tutor in this subject. Wonderful, blue-eyed Clive, the handsome older man I'd dreamed of throughout my sweltering adolescence; poor, trapped Clive, withered into a loveless marriage with a stony, flame-haired wife. He was my classical voice tutor, and during my three years of training he gave me frequent oral examinations.

"That's disgusting," said Hélène with a sudden maniacal cackle.

"But true," I said. "Seriously, though, I don't think you can be taught to act, any more than you can be taught to be a good lawyer. You can be taught the *subject*, and you can be shown the raw materials, but as far as getting up and doing it goes... that comes from inside." I tapped my sternum just above where I imagined my heart should be.

Hélène nodded sagely at this. "Absolutely," she said.

We lapsed into another warm silence, and smiled at one another. Hélène looked up at the ceiling and let out a prolonged sigh, then turned to face me.

"Why can't it be like this with dad?" she said in a far away voice. "Why are we the only ones who like each other?"

I had no answer for that, but I knew what she meant, and suddenly I was startled by the past. Had we really been those two awful teenagers locked in mortal combat over a ten pound note; who slapped, kicked, punched and bit their way to an uneasy truce? It seemed impossible.

We sat there in the kitchen for some time, leaning against one another in a wordless communion, and listened to the

118

wind in the trees outside.

"Mum used to love that noise," I said, waving my arm in an all-encompassing gesture. "She always said that the sound of wind in trees was like a distant river."

"Yes." Hélène was silent for a while, her face thoughtful. Then she linked her arm through mine and looked at me. "What are you thinking?" she said.

"About the last time I saw her," I said.

"When was that?"

"Before I went away with that touring theatre company," I said, becoming wistful. "She was well then, or reasonably well. 'Still going up and down', as she would say." I smiled at the memory. "That's what she always used to say when I asked her how she was. Still going up and down. She meant her stomach, of course, but it was her way of saying she was still alive, too." I looked down at the table top. "I miss her so much," I said. The words felt strange in my mouth, like copper. I wasn't sure, but it might have been the first time I'd ever uttered them. "And I never said goodbye... I was too late."

"It doesn't matter." Hélène's voice was soft, quiet.

"It does to me," I said. "That's what made it all so empty. You don't know what it was like coming back like that, and wondering if I would get there in time. When I got home and saw all the lights on, I felt so... desolate... because I knew what had happened, and I knew I had missed her."

I conjured the image in my mind's eye – Ravencrag silhouetted against the night, with yellow light spilling out of every window, exorcising my mother's absence, blinding it away with light, whilst behind it the December sky mocked her passing with a necklace of fabulous stars.

"You could see those lights for miles, 'Lène, blazing all the way down the drive," I told her. "When we drew up, the taxi driver said, 'Christmas Party?', and I wanted to hit him. Who ever heard of a party with no music? It was awful. I can't remember what I said to him. Then he drove off and I was alone. I came inside, and there was just silence, and I wanted to turn round and run away again. I'd thought there would at least be *somebody* home, but there wasn't, and I didn't know where you had gone. And when you came back, much later, bleary and drunk, nobody said anything! Nobody said the words. Nobody said, 'Kate has died.' It was terrible." My voice had fallen to a whisper. "I wish I'd seen her one last time!"

"No," Hélène said, shaking her head. "Believe me, Pip, you're lucky you have the good memories of Kate. Mine are nastier. You wouldn't want to swap, I assure you."

"Why?"

"Because I had to watch her dying. Peritonitis can be slow, and painful. In the end she was reduced to a husk, a tiny little paper skeleton pumped full of drugs to keep the pain away. She didn't know who she was, where she was, or who I was. And she was incontinent. She turned into this little yellow *thing* lying on a bed – not my mother at all."

Hélène looked up at the ceiling and pushed out her lower lip, pouting thoughtfully in exactly the same way as our mother used to.

"But you know what, Pip?" she said, "I'll swear she was waiting for you. I don't know how, but she knew you were coming home, and she was hanging on. She survived three days longer than the doctors expected, and I'm sure that's why."

"That makes it worse," I said. "Just a few more hours, and... "

"You wouldn't have recognised her, Pip. Keep the memories you have and be grateful." Hélène gave me an

120

encouraging smile, and let another silence fall. "And what about you?" she said after a moment, looking at me with her tired eyes. "How is it going with dad?"

"Not so bad, I suppose. We ignore each other most of the time," I said. "I think I'm getting used to the Creeping Jesus thing at last, but it's all very difficult. He's convinced that God has cured him."

My sister raised her eyes to the heavens. "And how is he really?"

"Annoyingly, rather better than he was," I told her. "Of course, he's very tired and sits in his chair all day, but he doesn't sleep as much as he did a week ago. And he actually seems stronger. He can manage the stairs on his own again."

Hélène dipped her head and sipped at her tea. "That was the big issue when Harry phoned me for help," she said. "He said he was fine so long as he could do that." She looked up at me. "Does this make you redundant?"

"In a way. But it's such a weird disease, 'Lène. People can look nearly dead one day, then healthy as a horse the next. And three days after that they might be dead. He's iller than he thinks."

"And now he thinks he's not ill at all," my sister deadpanned.

"A peach, isn't it?" I said.

"How's his weight?"

"I can lift him up with one arm," I said. Then, "Do you want to go and see him? You don't have to. He doesn't know you're here."

"I may as well," Hélène said without enthusiasm.

"I'll see if he's asleep," I said, and glanced at my watch. "He usually is by now."

I went upstairs and listened at his door. His slow, regular breathing confirmed my prediction and I returned to the kitchen to tell my sister.

"Good," she said when she learnt of her reprieve. "He'd only want to know why I was here."

I nodded, shivering as I stood in the cold kitchen. "Shall we go through to the sitting room," I suggested. "It's warmer in there."

"Why not?" my sister said, and led the way down the corridor.

The room was stifling in comparison to the rest of the house, which had remained unheated since our chilly childhood. At once we relaxed, like melting dolls, engulfed in our respective armchairs in front of the black Norwegian stove. Instantly torpid, I stared up at the gaudy cuckoo clock above Hélène's chair.

"Actually, there is something I want to tell you about dad," I told her.

"What?"

I hesitated, feeling selfish for mentioning it. She didn't need to hear of Harry's confessions. I knew perfectly well that the old cliché of 'a problem shared' was a huge lie.

"It's a little bit — I don't know if you're in the right frame of mind for it," I said, hedging.

"Don't say that," she complained, lighting yet another cigarette. "You've got to tell me, now that you've mentioned it."

"All right. But I warn you, it's a cracker."

I got up and slipped Harry's tape into the machine. I'd been carrying it around in my pocket for the last four days, afraid that Harry might find it if I left it anywhere in the house, unguarded.

"Listen to this," I said, and returned to my chair.

I watched her expression shift from curiosity to alarm, and then utter indignation, as my father's chilling voice relentlessly, inexorably denounced us. For some time after

122

the tape finished she said nothing, but sat back in her chair, her mouth part-open like a corpse, and stared into the middle distance.

"Where the hell did you get that?" she said at length.

"I found it in the attic," I told her. "In Kate's tape recorder. It was in a box, hidden away in the corner, along with her sketch books."

"I can't... I just can't believe he *said* that," Hélène stammered. "It's — "

"I hate him," I cut in, and for the first time in my life I thought it might actually be true. "In that tape," I said, pointing over my shoulder towards the machine, "he has confirmed every suspicion and prejudice that I ever had about him."

"Like what?"

"That he never loved us!" My voice came out louder than I had intended, high and cracking.

"You can't say that, Pip."

"I can, 'Lène. You should have been here that last summer, when Kate was ill. He never lifted a finger for her. Not once." I warmed to my subject, drawing on the bitter memories. "I remember one time, she wanted to go to Barringham House, the one with the famous rhododendron garden that goes on for miles. You know how she loved rhododendrons and azaleas."

My sister gave a faded smile and nodded.

"I'd left Bristol Old Vic in the March, and it was a couple of months after that – just when the gardens would have been in full bloom. But Harry refused to take her. I mean, he actually sat and watched the racing on tv instead of driving her a paltry thirty miles down he road for the afternoon. I'd have been willing to take her, but of course the car wasn't insured for me – surprise, surprise."

"That's awful," said Hélène. "What sort of person could – "

"He knew she was dying," I went on. "He knew that it would be her last chance to see those gardens, yet he still couldn't bring himself to do it. I never understood it then, but perhaps I do now."

"It's like the Union Jack ball," Hélène mused, and she laughed a bitter laugh. "God, I haven't thought about that for years!"

The summer I was four, Hélène and I had been given a ball to play with – a football-sized plastic ball with a Union Jack painted on it. It was the era before we started fighting, and we were happy to share it, inventing games together. It was our favourite toy, far more precious to us than many more expensive gifts – for reasons I can no longer remember – and in the way of children, it assumed enormous importance in our lives. We decided it had magical properties, and we took it everywhere with us. Naturally, it accompanied us on our annual seaside trip to Cromer, where it was blown into the sea and carried off by the current. Our father, lolling only feet away like a small pink slug, had refused to rescue it for us.

"I hated him for days after that," Hélène smiled.

"Me too," I said. It was one of my earliest, most vivid memories, and attached to it was a vague sense of anguish, letdown, and rejection. "Or I thought I did. Now, of course, I'm sure. And I think the feeling's mutual."

My sister looked at me with mild surprise. "Why should he hate you?" she said.

"Because I'm not the son he wanted," I said. "He gave up on me the moment he found out I was gay."

"But still... " Hélène began, but the sentence died in her throat, and I drew a perverse pleasure from the fact that she hadn't refuted my statement.

"And also because I was the one who argued with him," I added.

My sister gave me a long look. It was a look that told me she required an explanation.

"We argued a lot, 'Lène, after you left home," I told her. "Over just about everything. Some of those scraps got out of hand. It wasn't a happy time."

"You always were one for a good row," Hélène smiled, and suddenly her face flushed.

"What's the matter?" I said.

Hélène put her hands to her face, a gesture of embarrassment. "I was remembering that terrible set-to we had, just there!" She pointed towards the doorway, the scene of the Ten Pound Fight, all those years ago.

It was New Year's Eve, the year I was fourteen, and the family had gathered in the sitting room to indulge in our usual moribund end-of-year vigil. This involved staying up until midnight, always a struggle for most of us, whilst watching Kenneth McKeller and Moira Anderson chattering away on tv, then sipping a glass of sweet sherry as Big Ben chimed twelve, wishing one another a hasty and insincere Happy New Year, and staggering off to bed.

Hélène, then eighteen and in the full flood of her first major relationship, had been invited to a party elsewhere, which was sure to be more interesting than seeing the New Year in Winter-style. It was her first serious party, and she had spent all day getting ready. She had locked herself in her bedroom for hours.

My mother and I – minus Harry, who was still making last-minute finishing touches to the yard, which was due to open for business the following day – were watching a bad James Bond film when she came into the sitting room to show us her dress. It was sumptuous, with folds of plum-coloured material which fell to the floor from a tight waist, and scintillated when she moved.

Her hair was loose, and hung about her like a commercial for shampoo. She looked like a goddess. This was something of a transformation for Hélène. We had never seen her out of jeans or filthy jodhpurs, which she wore with outsized second-hand mens jumpers, and most of the time she looked like a stable-hand. But now she was a film star. We both stared at her with our mouths open.

"How do I look?" she asked, twirling around near the door.

"Perfect," said Kate with a broad smile. "You should wear dresses more often."

"Mu-um," Hélène sighed.

"Are you off now?"

My glamorous sister nodded and opened her small clutch bag, which I knew to be full of mysterious, girly things because I had peeked inside it once before. She rummaged about in it for a while.

"Damn," she said, "I haven't got enough money for the taxi."

Harry had long ago ceased to drive any of us anywhere, even though the house was completely isolated and was miles from civilization, on the grounds that he was not a public service. He didn't seem to care that this would result in my sister taking lifts with strangers, or walking alone in the dark, if she couldn't afford other transport. Perhaps he reasoned that nothing bad would happen in deepest rural Norfolk.

Hélène clicked her tongue in annoyance, then looked up from her clutch bag and settled her eyes on me. I knew that look. It meant trouble.

"Fy?" she said in her most pseudo-innocent, wheedling voice, "have you got that money?"

"What money?"

"The ten pounds I lent you before Christmas."

I looked at her with suspicion. At fourteen, I was short of funds, and had found it hard to scrape up enough money to buy Christmas gifts. Hélène had lent me ten pounds to see me *through, and I had paid her back immediately after Christmas with some of the money I had received as presents. Hélène must have forgotten this in all the frantic festivities.*

"I've already given it back to you," I said.

"No you haven't."

"I have," I said. "Of course I have."

"This is typical," my sister complained. She turned to my mother, and appealed for support. "You know damn well you didn't give it to me. You're just trying to wriggle out of it."

"I am not!" I cried in righteous indignation, and rose from my chair to stand facing her. She was six inches taller than me, and intimidating. "I gave it back to you ages ago," I said.

"Filthy little liar," she spat. "That's the last time I lend you any money. Give it to me now. I can't get a taxi if you don't. You'll ruin everything, like you always do."

"But I've paid it back already," I yelled into her face. "Why should I pay you again?"

My mother was used to our screaming matches and wasn't going to get involved. From the corner of my eye I could see her doggedly focusing in on Sean Connery as he performed tricks with a cunning wristwatch. She, who so disliked confrontation of any sort, was blotting us out.

"Are you going to give me the money, or not?" Hélène said. I could see her choler rising.

"Why should I?" I countered.

We could both tell this was going nowhere. But then Hélène raised the stakes with a well-struck slap that caught me about the face like a whiplash.

"Liar!" she said. "Thief!" she added as a second blow rasped my other cheek.

"No I'm not," I screamed, and launched myself at her, trying to get a purchase on her hair.

And with that, words became redundant. Instead, we rhythmically punched and kicked one another, locked in a dreadful pugilistic embrace. I grabbed hold of her lip with my hand, and pulled until she screamed. In return, she sank her teeth into my shoulder, drawing blood even through my clothes. We were both hot and tearful, but not crying, our breath ragged and atavistic.

"Will you stop that!" Kate boomed from the sofa behind us, but we were lost to our fury and continued unabated.

"Hélène! Philip!" she called again, but her voice was more frightened than commanding, and had no power to stop us.

Just as I landed a double-handed blow to the side of my sister's head, which had her staggering against the door, our mother grabbed us both by the hair and pulled hard. I felt a tearing sensation in my scalp as a clump of hair was uprooted, and I stood staring at my sister, who had received similar treatment.

"Stop it now," my mother shouted. And we did.

I turned round and looked at my mother, who was trembling, then turned back to Hélène. "I did give it to you," I blurted through thick lips. "I really did."

"When?" My sister's eyes were dark.

"About three days ago. I don't remember when exactly. But we were in the hall, by the phone. You must remember."

"No, I don't," she said, giving me a disbelieving stare. "But if you're not going to give it to me, then you're not." And with that she turned and left the room, fiddling with the straps of her dishevelled dress.

My mother stared at me across the suddenly quiet room as if I was another species. And perhaps I was.

"I didn't start it," I shrugged, and looked at the floor.

Five awkward minutes later, she went to find Hélène, to lend her the money for a taxi.

For my own part, I felt thwarted. I hadn't wanted to win the fight, I had wanted to be vindicated. As it turned out, I wasn't sure exactly what the outcome was, and it left a peculiar sensation in my stomach, like hunger.

"Yes. That's where we peaked," I told my sister as we stared down at the carpet, almost expecting some evidence to remain there. "But we never fought again, did we? I never understood why."

Hélène looked at me, an expression of discomfort on her face. "I can tell you exactly why," she said.

"Yes?"

Hélène hesitated for a moment. "You have to promise not to be annoyed, first," she said.

"Okay," I shrugged.

"It's because I realised that you were right half way through the fight."

"What?"

"You promised not to get annoyed," my sister reminded me. "But yes, half way through the fight, I began to think that you might have paid the money back after all. Of course, I was in too far by then, so I had to carry on with it. And then you said something – I can't remember what – and I knew at once that you really *had* paid me back. And it suddenly seemed too ridiculous for words that we could get so violent, so nasty, over a misunderstanding like that, and I vowed never to do it again. I mean, we weren't children, were we? I must have been eighteen. Old enough to know better."

"Why didn't you say something at the time?"

"I felt too stupid!" my sister told me. "And admitting it would have been worse." She looked at me with unreserved contrition. "Do you forgive me?"

I smiled. "Perhaps I deserved it, after the Jasper fiasco," I told her.

When Harry had set out to buy a horse, ostensibly for Hélène, the condition was that I should agree with her choice, as it would be handed on to me once I grew into it. This had placed too much power in my hands, at precisely

129

the time when I sought to hurt my sister in every possible way. As we had toured the area, peering into summer fields at sturdy young horses being put through their paces by eager vendors, I vetoed every one of Hélène's choices, including several that I genuinely liked, simply in order to be perverse. In the end Harry, grown impatient, chose Jasper – a horse neither of us wanted.

"Although he was a bit of a gem, in the end," Hélène said in a wistful voice. "Harry could always spot a good horse."

"Yes," I said.

Hélène paused for a moment, and stared down at her lap. "Of course, there was another reason why we stopped fighting," she said with a smile.

"What?"

My sister glanced at me with a rueful expression. "I grew up. I decided to forgive you for being a better horseman than me. That's what it was all about, really, wasn't it?"

"I don't know."

"I think it was," she said, and nodded to herself.

We lapsed into thoughtful silence, and I put on some of Harry's ancient music which warbled in the background as if it was coming from another era.

"Have you had any sign of work since that *Top Withins* job fell through, by the way?" Hélène said after a while.

"Uh... Did I tell you about this new telly series, *Rat Trap*?" Hélène shook her head. "Oh. Well, it seems I'm quite close to a good part in that. One of the regulars. I've got a casting for it on Friday, actually, so keep all appendages firmly crossed for me." I bobbed about in my chair, getting excited again. "It's a much better job than that cruddy old musical," I told her. "Much more me."

Hélène laughed. "Look at you!" she said, and shook her

130

head in wonder. "You have to be so hopeful and resilient to be an actor, don't you? I could never do it."

I shrugged. "You have to keep believing that next time it will be you," I said.

"Rather like the Lottery."

"Yes. And the odds for getting work are about the same."

Hélène smiled, then glanced down at her watch. "Oh god, it's gone nine," she said. "I'd better get on home otherwise Ewan will panic."

"How is he?"

"Fine. Still working all hours at the laboratory. Still enjoying it. And now Bryony has decided she wants to be a research scientist, too."

I smiled. Bryony had a different career planned every time I saw her. She had even flirted with acting – for all of a week.

"Paul's still intent on going to Cambridge," she added.

"A happy family," I laughed. "How did you manage to turn out so *normal*?"

We left the sitting room and meandered up the corridor, towards the front door, our shoulders hunched against the creeping cold of the house.

"And how is *your* life, little brother?" Hélène asked.

"Complicated, as usual," I told her.

"That's okay," she said, nodding with sisterly approval. "There's nothing wrong with that. Somethimes I think I'm *too* normal."

I shook my head. "I could do with a little normality just now," I sighed. "Callum's disappeared."

"You mean 'disappeared' disappeared?"

I nodded.

"Why didn't you tell me before?" My sister stared at me, wide eyed. "How can you be so calm about it?"

"It's already old news," I told her.

"What are you going to do?"

"Nothing I can do," I said. "I'm stuck up here until further notice. But my friend Chris said that he's done this kind of thing before, apparently. I'm not surprised. He lives off his nerves so much... All I can do is wait. See if he gets in touch."

Hélène gave me a concerned look and measured her words with care. "He won't have done anything... silly... will he?"

I smiled. "He won't have slashed his wrists, if that's what you mean," I told her. "He's got far too much ego for that."

Hélène opened the front door and hesitated, letting in the cold, damp air, then hugged me with those strong, swimmer's arms of hers, squeezing the breath out of my little body.

"Are you okay to drive after that dope?" I asked her. I was still feeling affected, and was looking forward to going to bed.

"Oh yes. I've sobered up completely," she told me. "Goodbye," she added, planting a kiss on my temple, the way Kate always used to. "Good luck on Friday."

"Thanks. Give my love to Ewan and the kids."

"I will," she said. "And phone me at once if there's any news of Callum. Or Harry."

"I will," I called as I watched her step round the side of the house, picking her way through the dark. Then I closed the door and shut out the winter night.

The next morning, Harry's cough returned at last, and I felt strange because I realised that I had been waiting for it. His face remained stoical as he sat in his chair by the stove, but behind his eyes there were clouds of confusion, and disappointment. As the day progressed, his breathing

132

became more laboured, turning wet and bubbly. It sounded almost as if he was smoking a bong. Even to my untrained ear it seemed far more severe than his previous bout of coughing.

"Do you need something for that?" I asked him, as the thin light outside began to fade. I was worried because the cough had presented itself so rapidly, and without warning, and had advanced so far.

My father seemed unconcerned. "The Lord will provide," he said, hacking into his handkerchief.

Scarcely concealing my irritation, I left the room and phoned the hospital. They suggested that I brought him in for observation. I told them I couldn't do that.

"Then come and get a tank of oxygen," the doctor advised.

I was extremely unwilling to leave Harry alone whilst I drove to the hospital and back, and I found myself tearing down those dark, familiar lanes like a rally driver, taking corners too fast and braking too hard. When I got there I loaded a canister of oxygen, a mask, and some rubber tubing into the back of the car and pelted back again. I felt like Doctor Kildare.

On my return, however, Harry beamed at me from his chair with a smug look on his face. His breathing had improved.

"It's Jesus," he told me.

I was annoyed, but comforted myself with the knowledge that at least I had some oxygen in the house now, for the next time. I knew there would be one. I had as much faith in the fact as Harry did in his recovery. Nevertheless, I didn't tell him about it. I didn't want him to think that I knew he was going to die. If he wanted to play Pretend, as he had with Kate, then who was I to interfere? So I waited until he was in bed before I unloaded it from the car and hauled it up to my bedroom. It felt like a bomb in my arms as I held the chilly metal to my chest. I leant the cylinder against the wall by my bed, and wondered how many false starts Harry would have, how many more times he would recoil from the brink, as he had the day I took him to the church. It made me tired just thinking about it.

On the morning of my audition, Harry seemed stable but more tired than before, like a flower which had passed its best. His clothes seemed emptier than usual, and his skin seemed thinner, more translucent, like the skin of a very old person. At breakfast, neither of us ate anything. Harry's meal consisted entirely of pills, which he washed down with tea, whilst I attempted, and failed, to eat a boiled egg. My stomach had closed down due to nerves.

"You're sure you'll be all right on your own?" I asked my father.

"I'll be fine, Fy. Don't worry about me."

"Maybe I should get Arthur to come and see you?" I offered.

"Don't fuss," Harry said. "It's only six hours, for Pete's sake. I can look after myself for six hours.

"Okay," I said, and wondered at my capacity to worry so much over a person I claimed to dislike.

My father swallowed one of his many capsules, then looked at me. "Concentrate on your audition, Fy. Put your mind to getting the part. Otherwise there's no point in your going. You've got to commit yourself."

I smiled. I had heard my father give this same pep talk to Hélène and me countless times in the past, as we prepared to take part in some hunter-trial or other – the only kind of riding that I'd actually enjoyed. Harry was big on commitment, and believed that competitions, jobs and races were all won in the mind before the door was opened, the gun fired, or the wire raised. To a degree, I concurred.

"Frankly, I'm terrified," I told him.

"Terrified is good," he announced.

"Not with acting," I said. "It should all be done from a point of rest."

"I thought nerves made you better."

"It doesn't work that way with me."

"Don't you get nervous before going on stage?"

"Not really. When actors say that, they generally mean they're excited. That's completely different."

Harry shrugged. "Good luck, anyway."

"You're not supposed to wish me luck," I joked. "You're supposed to tell me to break a leg." And I winced, knowing this was the fate which had ruined his career.

"I don't think I'll do that," my father said stiffly. "Good, old-fashioned luck will do."

I nodded and smiled. I was not a superstitious actor. "Thanks," I said, and went upstairs to get ready.

My agent had told me to wear a suit but I didn't have one with me at Ravencrag, so I left early, with a view to stopping off at my London flat first, where I could dress for the casting. Rule number one with tv is to dress as the character you are up for. Acting ability, sadly, is not considered important, and may be waived altogether if you are lucky enough to have a famous parent, or if you have previously excelled at some sport or other. I had none of these advantages, so I would have to rely on the superficial approach, which meant turning up looking exactly like their idea of Detective Spencer.

The day was moist, overcast, and misty, which helped to calm me as I drove south. I slid through the Norfolk countryside feeling quiet inside, my thoughts alternating between my father's failing health and the possibility of finally landing a serious job. But I was jolted out of my dream state when the engine died, without warning, twenty miles outside Cambridge.

I tried to stay calm, and took a cursory but futile peek under the bonnet, at the oily intestines beneath. I had never been knowledgeable or interested in cars and engines, and I hadn't the slightest idea what was wrong. I phoned the AA, and then spent an anxious half hour waiting for the repair man to arrive.

"It's your distributor," he cheerfully informed me, after he had inspected the engine with his expert eye. He was a squat, bald man, and was squeezed into an oil-stained suit of overalls several sizes too small. "But don't worry," he laughed, "it's easy enough to fix."

I glanced at my watch. I had given myself four-and-a-half hours to get to the audition – plenty of time to reach London, call in at the flat, and still get to Union House without rushing – but a delay was not good news. I would be cutting it fine.

"Will it take long?" I asked.

"No, you're in luck, mate. I've got VW spares in the van. I'll be twenty minutes at the most."

"Fine," I said, privately expecting it to take forty-five.

By the time I was back on the road, a crucial ninety minutes had elapsed. I hammered down the M11 from Cambridge like Nigel Mansell, but even so, as I neared the city which, so far, had failed to deliver me any of the things I had naively hoped for when I had first arrived there twelve years before, I realised that I was going to have to abort my plan. I did not have time to go home before the casting.

Angry and despondent, I crept through the thick midday traffic of central London and tried to decide what

136

to do. It was Hobson's Choice. Either I could go home and change, and turn up late for the casting, or I could arrive in the clothes I was currently wearing and be on time. But either way, I knew I had blown it. My body felt limp with disappointment. In a fit of Post-Modernist nihilism, I decided that it didn't matter anyway and drove straight to Shepherd's Bush. Even so, I was almost late.

I was neither nervous nor annoyed by this stage, and felt a kind of awful lethargy instead. Becalmed, I reported to reception, and took the lift to the appropriate floor, where I waited outside on a cold plastic chair. By the time I was called into the room I was actually yawning.

"Hello, Pip," said the director, a craggy-faced man whom I'd met at my previous two castings. "Thanks for coming in again."

"Hello," I smiled.

"This is George Watkins, by the way," said the director, indicating a middle-aged man seated beside him. He was wearing huge glasses and looked as if he would be more at home behind a computer terminal. "He'll be working on episode two, then episodes seven and eight – that's a two-parter – so he needs to look at you as well."

I nodded, making no attempt to take any of it in. The information was irrelevant. I was relieved that he didn't repeat the entire spiel about the ethos of the show, as he had on the other two occasions I'd met him.

He smiled at me. "I think what we'd like to do this time, is see you working on camera, if that's okay?" he said. "That's what we need at this stage. We've already heard you read."

I tried to mask my surprise at the request. Of course, they *had* heard me read, but not for this part. But the remark didn't fill me with hope. Rather, it alienated me, impressing on me once again the arbitrary nature of the awful business I was trapped in. The business that I both loved and hated, which I had no power to resist.

"No problem," I smiled, stifling the yawn which tried to escape my lips as I opened my mouth to speak. "Do you have some sides?"

The director passed me a sheet of paper which I didn't look at, and ushered me to the far end of the room, where two cameras were set up. As I positioned myself on the marks before them, I caught sight of myself in one of the monitors – a diminutive, unkempt man wearing grubby white 501s, lilac baseball boots, and a roll neck sweater – and I knew this was not a job I could possibly get. I was not the smooth Detective Spencer they were looking for.

"You're dark, aren't you?" the director mused as he studied my face on the monitor. "Mediterranean blood?"

"I think my family's secretly Jewish," I joked, making no attempt to behave like a suave detective. There was no longer any point.

The director laughed, and the Computer Nerd gave a lop-sided grin.

"Do you want a moment to look at the dialogue?" the Computer Nerd asked me.

"It's okay. I'll read it cold," I said. I'd discovered at drama school that I had a talent for this, and it always impressed people.

"Okay, Pip," the director said. "In your own time."

When I heard those dreadful, familiar words, a part of me automatically kicked into action, because somewhere inside I still wanted to give it my best shot, even if the odds against my winning the part were rising by the second. The least I could do was to prove that I could actually act, if only to myself. After all, I didn't know when I'd next have a chance to get in front of a camera. But another, more persuasive, part wanted me to get out of the room as fast as possible. Why, it rationalised, prolong a doomed audition?

I turned over the paper and held it at arm's length, so it wouldn't be in shot with me, and began to read. My voice sounded bored and flat. "'I hope this is good, Webster, because I'm a busy man. I take my leisure very seriously, and at this moment I'm being denied a cracking force four. So if you're wasting my time with another of your whimsical theories I'd like you to tell me now.'"

I stopped, and let my arms fall to my sides. The director and the Nerd muttered together for a moment whilst I stood there, awaiting their direction.

"That's good, Pip. Now, can you try it facing that way?" The director pointed towards the door.

I obliged, smiling to myself at their lack of interest in my artistic interpretation, and offered them my other profile. Then I read the piece again, sounding even more bored than I had the first time.

"That's fine. Now, will you ident that for us?"

I turned to face the cameras again. "This is Pip Winter," I said in my newscaster's voice, "and I'm with Jim Johnson. My last tv job was an episode of *The Bill*."

"Great. Now come and have a seat," said the director, and we returned to the chairs at the other end of the room.

I knew by the speed with which they whisked me through the standard availability questions, and by the way they were so attentive to me, that I hadn't got the job. It was ridiculous. I wanted them to tell me to my face, then and there, that I wasn't what they were looking for, but the charade dragged on for a further five minutes, with both parties making enquiries as if there was a distinct possibility that we'd be working together. I found it hard not to laugh.

It was still early when I left the building and found myself back on the street, and I felt light as a balloon as I gulped down the dank London air. The crushing disappointment at my failure, which was to come later on, was being held off temporarily by a taut, brittle relief to be out of the room. Of course, I didn't phone my agent. There would be nothing to say. *Hi, Jim. About the audition... Yes, I blew it big time. Can you fix me up with another one?* I shook my head and walked back to my car. As I slouched through the smoggy winter streets, I decided to call in at home. It would be wise to put in an appearance, to remind whoever may be watching that the flat was occupied. Living on the ground floor made me susceptible to break-ins, of which I'd previously sustained two, and I was keen to avoid the hat trick. There were also a few bits and pieces that I wanted to take back to Ravencrag – CDs and suchlike.

But it seemed I was too late. As I slipped my key in the front door, I noticed that the lock had been forced and then hastily repaired with glue and some poorly affixed screws. My stomach tightened. I pushed open the door and rushed in, but the place was dark, sepulchral, every curtain drawn. Warily, I went round the flat, systematically opening the curtains, but as I did so, each room was revealed to be in perfect order. Nothing had been stolen. In fact, the flat was tidier than it had been. The only exception to this was the kitchen, where a pile of foil containers – the remnants of several take-away meals – were scattered across the kitchen table along with many wine bottles. A pile of unwashed dishes lay in the sink.

When I entered the bedroom, my suspicions were confirmed. Callum was sleeping on the bed, fully clothed, with his mouth wide open. His presence in my flat finally explained how he had acquired Harry's phone number – an eventuality I suddenly realised I had half guessed all along. Angrily, I shook him awake, and as I did so I noticed that the clothes he was wearing were mine.

140

"What are you doing here?" I demanded as he looked up at me with bleary, unfocused eyes. "Why are you wearing my clothes?"

"Hi babe," he crooned, extending his arms to me for a hug. "Good to see you."

I stepped back, struck by the calm with which he was speaking, his lack of surprise at seeing me, and his ability to act as if he had not been missing for the past week.

Callum sat up, rubbed his face with his hands and yawned. "I knew you'd come looking for me," he smiled. "I knew you would."

"Why are you here?" I said at last in a cold voice. "What are you doing?"

"I wanted you," he said simply. "And you weren't around, so I decided to come here. If I couldn't be with you, then I wanted to be in your flat, with your things." He stroked the jumper he was wearing – my jumper – and smiled. "It smells of you," he said.

As I looked at him, a shiver went up my spine. This man, a man I thought I knew, was a stranger. And I would never be rid of him.

"You've got to stop all this," I told him. "This..." But words could not be summoned to describe what I meant.

"Were you worried about me?" Callum asked.

I thought for a moment.

"Yes." And I had been. But only a little. "I'm glad you're okay."

Callum rose from the bed and stood before me. In the half light he looked like a handsome statue, a living Moai from Easter Island. He took my head in his hands and kissed me full on the lips.

"I'm glad you came to find me," he murmured as he caressed the back of my neck with his hand. "I was waiting."

This was the moment at which I always buckled. After every one of our confrontations, Callum would use his body to break me down: I could take his hands in mine and gently, firmly tell him that the relationship wasn't working, that we should stop seeing each other; I could punch him in the face, push him physically out of the door and tell him to fuck off out of my life; I could explain in flat tones that it wasn't him, but me, who was at fault – but every time there would be teeth on a nipple, teasing with exquisite delicacy, a moustache between trembling buttocks and a moist, warm mouth finding in that cleft a yielding entry, like a thumb pressed into warm fruit, and I would allow myself to be bought by the touch of his tongue and the submissive pleasures of possession.

But not this time.

I pushed him away and took a step back, towards the wall. "No," I said. This was a man who had shackled me with emotional blackmail for two years. A man who owed me money. A man who had broken into my flat in order to wear my clothes. "Stop this. We've got to stop this."

"Why?" said Callum, trying to kiss me again.

"Can't you see it's not right. It's not normal."

"Fuck normal," said Callum.

Confused as I was by my conflicting emotions, I tried to put them in order. "But I *want* normal," I told him. "This stunt, this... vanishing act... was another of your games, wasn't it? Another test for me. And you think that this time, for once, I passed; that I came running down here to look for you. But I didn't. I had an audition this afternoon. That's the only reason I'm here."

"Oh."

With that, Callum seemed to collapse into himself. He wrapped his arms tight about his chest and sank back on to the bed, staring up at the ceiling. I allowed the silence to

142

roll round us. As I listened to my ragged breathing, I became aware that I was angrier that I had realised. And looking at Callum now, lying on the bed like a foetal husk, I felt not pity, but more anger.

"This is about that bloody holiday competition, isn't it?" I yelled. "Christ, Callum, don't you ever think? Don't you ever listen? How could I possibly get away from Ravencrag when my father needs constant supervision? I told you that before. So then you run off to play fucking hide and seek. How could I race around the country looking for you?"

I looked down at Callum, who had drawn his arms up over his head, as if to protect himself from my rain of words.

"I've had it this time," I told him, "I really have. I want you to go."

Callum remained inert on my bed. I grabbed him by the shoulders and pulled him up, where he stood before me on unsteady feet, saying nothing.

"Get out!" I said as I propelled him through the front door. "Go!"

He half-resisted me throughout the manoeuvre, then turned and leant all his weight against the door as I was trying to shut it. He managed to wedge his foot between the door and the frame, and we eyed one another through the sliver of open door for some moments.

"You couldn't lend me a few quid could you?" he whined. "Until Friday. I'm a bit short just now."

"Fuck *off*, Callum," I screamed, and heaved the door shut with my shoulder.

We both remained where we were, on either side of the door.

"I still love you, you bastard!" he shouted. "You can't stop me loving you."

"Just go, will you? Leave me alone. I don't want to be fighting all the time."

After five minutes, I heard his slow steps receeding down the street, and I allowed my self to sink to the floor, where I was assailed by a sudden bout of dry coughs. It took me a few moments to realise that I was crying.

The drive back to Ravencrag exhausted me. As I headed out of London, everything caught up with me all at once, and I developed a treacly headache which lodged behind my right eye like an incubus. Photosensitive migraine – a legacy from my mother. Before long, the headlights of oncoming vehicles, reflected up from the slick wet road, had me wincing in pain. I didn't have any pills with me, so drove the rest of the way home with my right eye screwed shut, wanting nothing more than to lie down in a dark room and sleep.

When I arrived back at my father's house, utterly spent, I headed straight for the bathroom and the comfort of several Paracetamol. I had just gulped a mouthful of icy water, to chase down the bitter pills, when my father's frail voice cut through the silence.

"Fy? Fy, is that you?"

The voice was small, distant, frightened, and sent a thrill of alarm through my heart. There was such need in it.

"Yes, it's me," I said, and headed down the corridor to the sitting room. But Harry wasn't there. I went back out into the corridor and called out, puzzled. "Where are you?"

"The stairs. I'm on the stairs," came the reply.

At once I knew something was wrong, and the insistent pounding in my head grew more intense as I hurried through the quiet house to my father. I found him sitting on the floor at the foot of the stairs, in the dark, with his back propped against the wall. His pale face almost shone in the gloom.

"What are you doing here, dad?" I said as I turned on the light.

Harry looked up at me like a child. "I fell," he told me in a thin voice. "I slipped on the stairs, and fell."

"How far?" I asked, alarmed.

"Only a few steps. But I hit my head. And I can't get up. I managed to get myself sitting, though."

I looked down at his head. A knot of dried blood nestled at his left temple, matting his short white hair.

"Let me see that," I said, and squatted down to look more closely at his wound. "I don't think it's too bad," I told him after a moment, "but you're very cold. How long have you been here?"

"I don't know. I've been asleep."

This alarmed me, having overtones of concussion. "Come on, let's get you warm," I said, and stooped to pick him up. For once he didn't resist me, and folded into my arms like a broken doll as I carried him through to the sitting room.

"Can you stand?" I asked him, about to lower him to the floor.

"I should think so. There's nothing broken. It was only my head," he said.

I supported him whilst he tentatively put his feet on the ground. Then he straightened up with a half smile. He could indeed stand.

"Sit by the fire and warm up," I instructed him, and drew his armchair closer to the Norwegian stove. Fortunately, the stove was designed to burn slowly for many hours without attention, and was still generating a good heat. "I'll get you a drink. What would you like?"

"Whisky," he replied as he shuffled over to the chair.

145

"Oh," I exclaimed.

I was surprised, because it was the first time he had requested alcohol since I had arrived, weeks before, and I'd somehow assumed that he was squeaky clean and tee total. I wondered if it was a bad thing to give people alcohol in these situations, but I didn't press the point. Neither could I remember if it would be good or bad to get him into a hot bath, and once again I felt inadequate as his nurse. I didn't have the first idea what I was doing. And I also felt tremendously guilty, because I was responsible for Harry's fall. If I had been here, if I hadn't gone to London, he wouldn't have fallen. It was my fault.

Not wishing to risk a bath, I wrapped Harry in a blanket as he sat in his chair by the fire, then gave him his whisky, which he clutched with his tiny claw hands.

"I think you should let a doctor check you over," I said as he sipped his drink.

Harry shot me a thunderous look. It was a look of warning, the look he used to throw out in advance of a blow when I was a child, but now it had no power over me.

"I'm fine," he said.

"Then you've nothing to worry about if you let a doctor see you," I retorted.

"The Almighty is my doctor," he replied.

"But he's not mine, and I'm responsible for you," I told him, exasperated. The pain in my head had got no better, and the vision in my right eye was blurring to extinction. "I'll call out Dr Daniels."

I rose from my chair and made for the door, but Harry called me back.

"Don't, Fy. Please." His tone was plaintive, beseeching.

"Why not?" I asked him.

Dr Daniels had been our family doctor for years. It was he who had encouraged Harry to seek help from his

146

children in the first place. Although not quite a friend, he had achieved the status of Christmas card terms with us. Surely he didn't count, with regard to Harry's phobia about the medical profession?

"I don't want him to see me like this," Harry said. "It's not normal."

"Like what? You're an old man who's fallen down stairs. What could be more normal than that? He must see it all the time."

"I tell you, I'm all right." My father's lips tightened into a straight, stubborn line.

In the face of such intransigence, I risked a compromise. "All right," I said, and sat back down again. "But if you have so much as a single bruise in the morning, I'm calling him out whether you like it or not."

"I shall be fine in the morning," said Harry, downing his whisky.

My father soon fell asleep, cocooned in his chair, with the light from the fire lending his pallid face an unnatural, healthy glow. I didn't think that this was a good sign. For all I knew he might have been suffering from concussion, or hypothermia, and I felt sure I'd read that in both cases one was supposed to keep the patient awake. Once again I sighed at my inexpert care, and a cocktail of emotions washed through me like a rising tide. It wasn't so easy to hate him after all. Hate was not the clean emotion I'd imagined, with sharp, smooth lines. It was serrated, with fragments of love, duty, and guilt embedded in it.

Gently, I carried him upstairs to bed. He weighed less in my arms than the oxygen tank I'd hauled up to my room four days before. As I passed the small, slitted turret window in the curving wall of the stairwell, cradling my tiny father against my breast, I had a sudden presentiment that Harry would never come downstairs again. It startled me, because the thought arrived whole, and with such clarity that I felt it had to be true. I tried to dismiss it as fanciful – I had never been one for psychic phenomena – but nevertheless it unnerved me, and I lay awake for some time fretting about it as my vice-like headache squeezed my brain.

The next morning, I looked in on Harry as usual and found him lying on his back, staring up at the ceiling with an expression I didn't recognise. His face, which had been so white since my arrival, had turned a livid purple, and he was coughing again – long rumbling coughs which bubbled up from his ruined lungs like hot mud.

I moved over to the bed. "Sit up," I told him, "you'll be able to breathe more easily like that."

"I can't," came the reply, a short gasp of words that barely escaped his lips.

Quickly, I sat him up, arranged his pillows behind him in a stack, then laid him back down. This helped a little, but not much. Then I went through to the bedroom and fetched the oxygen tank. Harry stared at me with his large, bush-baby eyes as I manoeuvred the tank to his bedside and began to fiddle with the tube and mask. I looked at the dials, perplexed, realising with dismay that I had no real idea how to work them, and for the umpteenth time felt thoroughly inadequate. After some experimental twisting of knobs, I managed to evince a hopeful hissing from the tank, and handed Harry the mask.

"Here," I told him, "breathe this."

My father was reluctant, but took the proffered mask when a further bout of weak coughs threatened to choke him. He pressed the plastic mouthpiece to his lips and inhaled like a cartoon character sniffing flowers, whilst I sat on the bed beside him.

After several minutes with the mask, he lifted it from his

148

face. "What's this contraption doing here?" he said, and nodded towards the cylinder.

"It was a contingency plan," I told him, "after the last time you had trouble breathing."

Harry looked at me, helpless. "I didn't know," he said.

"There's a lot you don't know," I said.

Harry nodded, and returned the mask to his face.

"I'm calling Dr Daniels now," I said, and rose from the bed. "I told you last night," I added, in answer to my father, who weakly flapped his hand in protest.

I rang the doctor and explained what had happened the previous night – how Harry had fallen, how I didn't know how long he'd been lying there, and how he wouldn't let me call anyone out. "I don't know if this new breathing problem is anything to do with that," I added.

"Indirectly, perhaps," the doctor told me. "When a body sustains a shock like that, especially a compromised body, it can begin to collapse almost instantly, even if the physical damage is negligible."

"I see."

There was a pause at the other end of the line.

"I think you should prepare for the worst," he said at last.

When I got back upstairs, Harry was looking a little better. He wasn't so purple, and he was breathing without the oxygen.

"I turned it off," he informed me when I gave him a questioning look.

"Dr Daniels is on his way over," I said, and sat down on the bed beside him.

"I don't think that's necessary, now," Harry said. "I feel much better."

"Until the next time," I replied. "Anyway, he's coming and that's that." I felt like a firm father admonishing a

149

child. "If nothing else, he can look at the lump on your head." I regarded his temple, still caked with blood because he hadn't let me anywhere near it. Harry had been in no state to clean it up himself. "I'm sure he'll think I'm a dreadful nurse," I mused.

When Dr Daniels arrived, Harry became strangely acquiescent, turning this way and that as requested, a model of compliance. He was no longer the rigid, resistant patient that I had been presented with over the past weeks, and I found it hurtful. It was a clear statement that it was *me* he resented, not the fact that he needed a carer, and my heart hardened towards him again, like fired clay.

Twenty minutes later, I was showing the doctor out. "Can we talk?" he said as we made our way to the front door.

I nodded, and we went into the dining room.

"It's not good, Pip," he told me once I'd closed the door behind us. "He really should be in hospital now."

"I know. But he won't go."

"You should insist. *I* should insist."

I shrugged.

"Then how about getting a nurse in?"

I shook my head. "I know what you're saying, but no. We agreed to do it like this at the beginning. He really doesn't want anyone else involved. I had enough trouble getting *you* here." I looked Dr Daniels in the face. "And whatever I may privately think," I added, remembering Harry's casual dismissal of our family as meaningful landmarks in his life, a denouncement to rival that of his beloved St Peter, "whatever I may privately think, I wouldn't feel comfortable about imposing on him. And let's be honest, a nurse, or even an entire hospital, can't save him now, can it?"

Dr Daniels regarded me with a dour expression. "All I'm

saying is that, in my professional opinion, home care is no longer sufficient. Your father needs constant supervision. He's going to need regular injections of drugs..."

"I know. But I'm still not taking him to the hospital."

We stood in the cold dining room, eying one another.

"In that case, you'll need these," he said, and scooped a large quantity of pills, some drip bags, IV needles, a small, strange-looking pump, and some vials of clear liquid from his voluminous bag.

"What are all those?" I said as he laid them out on the dining table for me to look at.

"Food supplements. Morphine. Drugs for the PCP. Strong stuff. We can pump him full of it."

"We?"

Dr Daniels cocked his head towards me. "Unless you know what you're doing with it all," he offered.

"No, I'd be glad of the help," I smiled, relieved beyond measure. "I just thought..." But I didn't know what I thought, and stopped.

Dr Daniels, who had seen me through my various childhood illnesses, whose cold hands had slid over my chest and back many times in diagnostic enquiry in decades past, stood before me like a benign statue. His pleasant, craggy face reflected a care-worn sixty years, but his eyes were the eyes of a child. He smiled.

"Let's just say that I understand this... illness," he said in a wistful voice. "I understand it. I really do."

And as I looked at this modestly good looking, never-married doctor, I finally understood what he meant. "Oh," I blurted, and blushed.

We went back up to Harry's bedside, and Dr Daniels fitted the small box-like pump contraption to my father's arm, deftly slipping an IV needle into a vein in the back of his hand. Harry did not protest, but he averted his eyes

151

from us.

"This will pump a regular dose at four hourly intervals," he told me as he fitted one of the clear vials into the machine. "It's easy to maintain. All you have to do is check on it and make sure it doesn't run out. If it does, then you replace the vial."

"Okay."

Once he had checked that everything was in order, I showed him out and we shook hands on the doorstep.

"Ring me if you need any help," Dr Daniels told me. "Or if a lump appears on his hand where the needle is."

"Thanks. I will."

Dr Daniels seemed reluctant to leave. He lingered on the doorstep and gave me another of those benign yet stern looks. "Now are you sure you can cope, Pip? Are you certain he's taking all his medication?"

I nodded, suddenly uneasy.

"Hospital really is the place for him now."

"I know what you're saying," I told him. "I'll think about it."

"Good," he smiled, and left.

Harry stopped eating that day. His appetite hadn't been very substantial at any point, but now he refused all offers of food. He would only drink, so I prepared him a rich mulch of pureed vegetables with added vitamins and nutrients that Dr Daniels had given me, but he hardly sipped at it. And he couldn't keep it down for long anyway. I was shocked and frightened by the swiftness of the onset of this new symptom. Perhaps it was a reaction to whatever Dr Daniels had pumped into him.

"You're going to need to be near the bathroom," I told my father that afternoon, as he lay weak from a combined fit of vomiting and coughing. "I'm going to move your bed downstairs, into the sitting room. It's warm there."

Harry's eyes were baleful. He knew what this meant. It was what he had done for Kate at the end. "All right," he sighed.

"I think it's best," I said, and scooped him into my arms and carried him downstairs, careful not to dislodge his new drip, where I sat him in a chair by the stove. Then I went back upstairs and dismantled one of the twin beds in my room, and carried it down to the sitting room piece by piece. It was hard work negotiating the narrow spiral stairs singlehanded, staggering downwards beneath the weight of the bed frame, and I worked up a good sweat. But I didn't mind. It was a welcome respite from the profound chill which had crept into my bones that morning as I'd sat beside Harry in his unheated bedroom.

I erected the bed round the corner of the L of the sitting room, near Harry's enormous leather-topped desk, which I thought might be useful as a bedside table. Also, from this vantage point there was a pleasant view through the large french doors at the far end. In good weather one could see the corner of Harebell paddock. He'd be able to see the horses. All in all, I felt it was an improvement on his bedroom.

Once I'd made up the bed I slid Harry between the sheets, where he lay quite still, like a frightened animal. Then I fetched his oxygen and all the pills that were usually stationed in his room, and put them on his desk with the others. The field of worn leather now resembled a small pharmacy, littered as it was with weird and wonderful tablets and lotions.

"What else do you need?" I asked him, as I surveyed the crowded desk.

"Nothing. I don't want anything."

"What about your glasses?" I said. "You might want to read something."

I went upstairs to fetch them without waiting for an answer. They looked bereft, lying there on the cabinet beside his empty bed, and it made me profoundly sad. The little lenses seemed vulnerable, somehow, and infinitely redundant without their owner. In that moment, I knew that when Harry died it would not be the loss of him that would silence me, but the sight of some trivial artefact such as his widowed glasses.

On my return, it occurred to me that my bedroom was upstairs at the other end of the house, and that I would not hear Harry if he were to want anything in the night. So I decided to sleep in a chair in the sitting room. It was so strange, dozing through my long vigil as the fitful sounds of my sick father drifted into my half-sleeping mind. The tables had turned. I was the parent and he was the child. Had Harry felt this way when I had whooping cough, aged four, and almost died?

I sent for more oxygen the next morning, because Harry was finding it harder and harder to breathe. He spent most of the time behind his mask, with his grey-lidded eyes half closed, and I was worried about what would happen if it ran out. His face had assumed the colour of the dying.

In the middle of the afternoon, however, he enjoyed a period of easier breathing. "How...did...it...go?" he suddenly gasped, a propos nothing at all.

I was taken aback. It was the first time he'd spoken since the previous evening. "What?" I said.

"The...aud...ition..."

I hadn't thought about it for two days – it had been driven from my mind by the weightier events of Callum, and my father's fall – and the wound of disappointment had already healed. The scar that remained was barely perceptible.

"Oh, the usual thing," I told him. "The 'We'll let you

know' routine. I didn't get it."

Harry turned his slow eyes to me. "You...never...know."

I nodded my head. "I do," I said. "I really didn't get it."

"We'll... see," my father gasped. He pointed heavenwards, and patted my hand with a papery palm.

That evening, Harry took a remarkable turn of improvement. His breathing returned to normal, and he wanted to get up. He even wanted to eat. I sat him in his armchair – I wouldn't let him out of the sitting room – and fed him two fish fingers and some mashed potato, which remained in his stomach for once. A blooming rash had appeared over one side of his face, but aside from that, he looked healthier that he had for a long time.

"I feel marvellous," he told me. "Praise!"

"Good," I said.

"The Lord is being merciful."

"Mmn," I said.

My tone must have conveyed my scepticism, because Harry threw me a jagged look. "What do you know?" he growled, with a trace of his old, belligerent voice.

I shrugged in reply, which seemed to irritate him even more.

"So now you're the expert?" he barked.

My father stared at me, with a steely glint in his eye stronger than seemed possible, coming from one so frail, and instantly I was spoiling for a fight. Surely he couldn't still believe that he was being cured? Not after the roller-coaster ride of the previous forty-eight hours. It was absurd. I didn't know where it came from – stress, perhaps, coupled with the disappointment of the casting – but I found words tumbling from my mouth almost without my knowledge:

"Yes, unfortunately I am an expert," I said, "because I've seen it all before. You're not the first, and you won't be the last. But I'll tell you who *was* the first. It was Rob."

My father looked at me, blank faced. "Rob?" he said.

"Surely you remember him?" I cried. "He's the one you threw out of the house, five years ago."

"I didn't throw him out."

"As good as," I said. "We were together over two years, and you never once asked after him."

My father waved a dismissive hand at me, and his famous sneer perched on his thin lips. "I can't keep track of all your friends," he said.

"He wasn't my friend, he was my lover," I said.

"I was employing a euphemism."

"A euphemism is a pleasant term for something offensive. There was nothing offensive about Rob."

My father heaved a great sigh, which signalled either contrition, irritation, or tiredness. It was impossible to tell which.

"That's always been your problem, hasn't it?" I went on. "You've been on at me ever since I told you I was gay."

It felt weird. Here I was, yelling at my dying father. I was supposed to be his carer, not his tormentor. It shouldn't be like this. But at the same time I didn't feel disappointed, or even guilty, that it was happening this way. I hadn't been naive enough to expect any form of reconciliation during my stay at Ravencrag, or to lay any ghosts. Of course, I couldn't speak for Harry.

"Is that what you think, Fy? You think that was the problem?" My father said.

"What else?"

Harry looked at me with his blotchy face. "This may come as a surprise to you, but the world does not revolve around the sexual proclivities of one Philip Winter," he said.

"You mean, you decided to pick on me for no reason at

156

all?" I said. "Because you simply didn't like me? That only makes it worse."

"There were other things."

"Like what? What could possibly explain twenty years of sniping, dad?"

Harry's face seemed to fold in on itself, a slow implosion which began with his mouth. He screwed his eyes tight shut and unleashed a long, jagged breath through gritted teeth, his hands balled up into fists.

"Christ!" he shouted, and the blasphemy reverberated around us like a bomb. "Have you always been this blind, you stupid boy? You threw it all away!"

The outburst contained so much anger, so much hurt, that I let out an involuntary gasp. "What?" I said.

"The horses, damn you! The horses! You could have really been someone. You had the gift, you had the hands. But no, that wasn't good enough for you. Not different enough. Too much like hard work. You had to go to London and be an actor. And look at you now. Nothing."

Harry's face wore the same closed expression it had worn the day I stopped riding. I could almost smell the saddles ranged in racks about me as we faced one another, bristling, in the tack room. I felt sixteen again, when he was the parent and I was the child.

It was August, the eye of the summer holidays in the year I sat my O levels, and I was due to hack out with Hélène, on Jasper. To date, the entire summer had been characterized by a lingering inner sense of inevitability, as if I were accelerating towards a precipice. Lately I'd been growing tired of the endless work surrounding the riding of horses: the grooming, the mucking out, and the upkeep of the tack itself – which needed to be polished and soaped with monotonous regularity – not to mention the actual tacking-up of Jasper, who never stood still for long and always made the task difficult. I knew something had to give sooner or later. It wasn't as if the pleasure of the hack would render these unpleasant activities worthwhile. I'd had enough of everything, including the riding. I couldn't cope with Harry and Hélène, and their boundless enthusiasm. I found it stifling, and I knew I had to stop.

As I walked to the tack room that afternoon, I felt quiet inside. Harry hadn't spoken to me all day. He'd been avoiding me ever since I'd wandered into the sitting room two days beforehand and informed the assembled family, a propos nothing at all, that I was gay. I'd had to do it. It had been building up inside me for weeks, like a slowly inflating balloon, until the information was forced out of me by the pressure within. I hadn't waited to gauge their reactions to my news, and fled back to my bedroom. Now it seemed obvious: Kate and Hélène were unmoved – which, obtusely, I found annoying – and Harry was freezing me out, clearly outraged.

I crossed the yard feeling terribly different and changed, as I had for the past two days. I was sure that I was radiating homosexuality for all the world to see. Arthur raised an arm in salute as I passed, from the door of a nearby stall, and I nodded back.

"Goin' out, are you?' he called.

"That's the plan," I said.

"Jasper's in Primrose," Arthur said. "I'll fetch him in for you if you like."

"You'll do no such thing," my father said, suddenly emerging from the far end of the tack room. "Philip can bring him in himself, if he wants to hack out."

Arthur looked uncomfortable, undecided as to what to do. "It's no trouble," he said.

"And it's no trouble for Philip, either. Off you go, Fy."

But I had already gone into the tack room to fetch my saddle and bridle. I was in the habit of transporting them to Jasper's

158

box, where he would usually be waiting for me, courtesy of Arthur.

My father rushed past me and pushed his face into mine. "What do you think you're doing?" he demanded.

"Getting Jasper's tack."

"You'd better get him in first. Arthur isn't going to do it for you."

I remained where I was, silent and sullen. My arms were full of tack, with my saddle slung over my right arm. "In that case, I'm not sure I can be bothered," I said, moving over to the saddle racks in order to replace my equipment. "Perhaps I won't hack out after all."

At this, my father's face grew purple with rage, and his little body shook. "Who the fuck do you think you are?" he shouted, his face only inches from my own. "Little Lord Fauntleroy? This isn't a holiday camp, sport. It's a yard, and that means work. Muck-raking, leading out, grooming, and tacking-up. You don't just snap your fingers and expect Jasper to appear, ready to go. Arthur works for me. He's not your fucking batman."

"I never said he was."

"Then stop treating him like one."

"I don't," I screamed. "The only person round here who treats people like slaves is you!"

Harry swung a heavy blow at me then, and it caught me on the side of the head with such force that it made my ears ring. "You little shit," he said.

I stood there, daring him to hit me again, and then, very deliberately, I let my armful of tack fall to the floor in the deep silence. The snaffle bit rang out against the concrete floor as it fell, then the heavy saddle crashed down on top of it.

"Right. That's it," I said, relishing the sudden weightlessness of my arms. "I'm not interested any more. If that's what it takes, I'm just not interested." And I walked away.

"Come back here and pick up this saddle," my father yelled,

159

but I was already walking across the yard. "I"m warning you, Fy," Harry cried, his voice echoing amongst the stalls, "if you're not prepared to put in the work, I'm not prepared to let you ride. Full stop."

"Good!"

"Are you going to pick up this saddle, or not?" Harry bellowed, his voice rising in agitation.

"Take a guess," I replied, and began to walk back to the house.

I was almost at the garden gate when Arthur caught up with me. He dropped his small brown hand on my shoulder with the lightest of touches, and I turned to face him.

"You got any idea what you're giving up, boy?" he said in that slow quiet voice of his.

I shrugged. "It's not my thing," I told him.

Arthur looked at me, his face inexpressibly sad. But there was agitation there too, quickening his eye.

"Listen here, boy," he said, "your dad won't say it for 'e's too damn proud, but I will. In all my time I never saw a more capable pair of hands on a jockey. Thaa's how you won all those cups for hunter trialin'. You got dream hands, boy, and you know it. There's a great future for you out there, with the horses. Can't walk away from that, can you?"

I looked him in the eye for a moment, then began to turn away, back towards the house.

"You don't understand," I told him. "I'm really not interested." And I went on into the house, my heart lighter than it had been for weeks.

"You threw it all away," Harry repeated, waving his tiny hand in another dismissive gesture. "All that talent. Such a waste."

I looked at him as he sat in his armchair, the very picture of a bitter little man. "No," I said. "It wasn't. Because I hated it. It would only have been a waste to give up if I'd

160

enjoyed it, if I'd wanted to succeed at it. But I didn't. To carry on would have been pointless. Besides, Hélène was as good as me, and she lived for it. Why didn't you groom her for racing instead?"

"Don't fish, Fy. You know she's never been half the horseman you were. And she was always going to be too big, in any case."

A silence fell between us as I tried to absorb the meaning of what Harry had just said.

"So it's all because I refused to ride?" I said at last.

Harry shrugged. "What else?"

I stared at my father in bewilderment. I had always believed that the fulcrum which balanced our mutual displeasure was my sexuality, but now he was inferring that it was not so. I didn't know what to make of this, or even if I should believe it. If it was true, then the stone upon which I had always sharpened the axe of my resentment had suddenly been removed. How would I keep its blade keen now, I wondered?

Harry's health remained vulnerable for the next two days, and as time passed I felt a growing edge of nerves: I was anticipating the inevitable, a weight I carried with me at all times and which made me feel inexpressibly tired. But at least during that period there was something to draw strength from. With hindsight, I felt good about Callum. It seemed that I had finally said no to him and meant it. I had not phoned him; I had not succumbed to his corporeal charms and taken him back. And he had not called me. I felt, viscerally, that this time we could stay apart, and I congratulated myself on that.

But there were other problems. It was now three days since my abortive casting for *Rat Trap*, and I still hadn't phoned my agent. I was too embarrassed by my failure. Of course, I knew I ought to call him, and guilt-trip him into securing me another audition, but somehow I couldn't bring myself to do it. Instead, I buried my nose in *Bleak House* and sat by my father, who had begun to develop further difficulty in breathing.

My eyes skimmed the discoloured pages – it was an old, second-hand edition which offered up a slightly musty smell – but I couldn't take any of it in. I was too busy listening out for any subtle changes in the rhythm of Harry's laboured breaths. He was unable to sit up now, let alone get out of bed, and lay there beneath his mask looking bluish grey, sucking greedily at the pure oxygen. As I watched him, I knew that I was looking at the shadow of death. He would not bounce back this time. It seemed that Harry knew it too because his eyes, which looked huge in his emaciated face, contained fear and acquiescence in equal measure.

The morning wore on, inching away to the metronome of my father's feeble lungs, and I continued to read the same passage of my book over and over again. It was like some sort of mental torture. Eventually the cycle was broken by the shrill, vulgar call of the telephone. Grateful for the interruption, I put down my book and answered it.

"Hello?" An involuntary shiver ran through my body as I stood in the chilly hall, clutching the phone.

"Pip. It's Jim Johnson here."

"Oh, I was going to call you," I told my agent limply, and felt a flush of embarrassment redden my face. "Sorry. I've been a bit tied up."

There was a pause at the other end of the line. "Quite so," my agent said in a sober voice, "but I've got some news that I think might cheer you."

"Not another call for *Les Misérables*?" I said in my most laconic drawl.

162

"Very funny, I'm sure. No, it's *Rat Trap*."

"They want to see me *again?*" I exploded. "They've got some neck."

"No, no, no," my agent cooed. "Of course they don't, you chump. They've offered you the part!"

I didn't miss a beat. "For a moment there, I though you said they'd offered me the part," I quipped.

"I did. They have."

I was dumbstruck. Surely they couldn't possibly have been impressed by my super-casual appearance and attitude, let alone my tedious rendition of the sides I'd been asked to read. Besides, three days had elapsed since my casting. No news was usually bad news in my line of business.

"But I... It was days ago... How the...?" I trailed off, lost for words.

"You know them," my agent explained, "wanting everything yesterday one minute, then dragging their heels the next. This is the BBC we're talking about."

"I can't believe it. The casting went so badly."

"Apparently they were impressed by your character work."

I laughed out loud. "What character work?" I cried. "I didn't have time to change into the right gear because the car broke down. I looked like a scarecrow and I read like a moron. That's why I didn't phone you. I screwed the whole thing up." I knew this was not the sort of thing an actor was supposed to admit to his agent, but I couldn't help myself. "I don't understand," I told him.

"Detective Spencer is something of a sailor," my agent explained. "To the point of tedium, apparently. It's his sub-text in the show. They thought you looked nautical."

"I see," I said, and nodded to myself. True to casting

form, I'd got the job because I'd looked right, even if it had been completely by accident.

"I take it you accept?" my agent went on.

"Of course."

"Good. I'll get on to them. By the way, it seems you were the last to be cast, so you'll be starting more or less immediately. They're talking about next week for initial filming."

"Okay, fine," I said, not really listening. I was too caught up in the elation of it all to be bothered with the details. Now, at last, here was the break I felt I so richly deserved. "That's fine," I repeated.

"And they want you to go down for a wardrobe call as soon as possible. They were talking about today."

"I can't do that," I said.

"Of course you can't," my agent agreed. "But do you think you could manage tomorrow morning?"

I thought for a moment. Harry was far too ill to be left alone now. "I don't know," I said. "I can't leave my father."

"Ah."

"But I'll sort something out, Jim. Can I call you back?"

I phoned Hélène on her mobile number.

"What is it?" she blurted when she heard my voice. "Is it dad?"

"Not exactly. I've got that tv job I was telling you about."

My sister let out a controlled shreik of excitement. "Oh, well done, Pip," she squealed. "I'm so pleased."

"But there's a problem. I have to go to a wardrobe call tomorrow morning. And I can't leave Harry."

"I'll come up this evening, then," Hélène offered without hesitation. "I can look in on him for you. That way you can travel down tonight instead of having a hideous early drive in the morning."

"Will that be all right?"

164

"Perfectly. I have a hearing tomorrow, but it doesn't start until the afternoon, and I can read my notes just as well at Ravencrag as I can at home."

"Thanks, 'Lène. You're a star."

"You'd do the same for me," she told me, embarrassed by my gratitude.

I phoned my agent and told them I'd sorted it out. Ten minutes later he confirmed that I was expected at nine thirty – why was it always so early? – the following morning.

I went back to my father, who was lying in bed like a bundle of sticks. His bright eyes followed me as I moved to his side.

"That was my agent," I told him, a dance-drug smile hovering on my face. "I got that part after all."

Harry patted my hand and pointed upwards with a smile. "It's Jesus," he mouthed through his mask.

I sighed. It seemed that I was not to be given the credit even for this, my greatest achievement so far. God was responsible for everything. But for once I didn't let Harry prick the bubble of my euphoria, as he had so often in the past, and I remained self-contained and buoyant.

It felt wrong, being excited and happy whilst my father lay in bed beside me, moving closer to death with every breath, but I couldn't help it. The actor's disease had taken control of my body. I began to imagine what I would do with a large regular salary; I began to wonder if there was a chance that my character would be promoted from minor status to major; I began to wonder if I'd get my picture in the What's On TV magazines. I couldn't stop smiling, and had to fight the urge to burst into song. Kate had always done that when excited – an ecstatic ululation of song would erupt from her mouth without warning whilst walking up the corridor, making a cup of coffee, or even reading a book. Usually it was a random snatch from *Irene*, *South Pacific*, or *Joseph*, her favourite shows. I had inherited those same compulsive-singing genes, but with me it was always something from a show I'd been in. This time, in deference to my father, I managed to curb my enthusiasm and contented myself with a warm inner buzzing which remained with me, like a precious secret, throughout the afternoon.

As promised, Hélène arrived at about seven.

"Tea?" I offered, and she nodded.

I briefed her about Harry as I got it ready. "You won't have to do anything," I assured her. "You could try to get him to eat something, but he probably won't." I stopped and looked at her. "But what am I telling you this for? You've done it before."

She nodded, with a grim expression. "Déjà Vu," she said.

I took her in to see Harry, who seemed unsurprised that his large daughter had come to the bedside.

"I've got to go to London," I told him, "so Hélène's going to stay with you for the night."

My father either didn't hear, or didn't care, and gave no sign or answer. Perhaps he was relieved that my sister was going to be looking after him, rather than me.

"See you tomorrow," I said.

The drive down to London was uneventful but as I let myself into the flat my chest tightened at the prospect of finding Callum there again. What would I do then? I had no idea. But the flat was empty and I relaxed. Half an hour later, however, there was a knock at the door. Not a polite can-I-come-in knock, but an aggressive thumping which made my heart gallop.

"Who's in there?" came a high male voice. There were more thumps on the door.

I stood in my hallway, perplexed and dismayed, and

hoped this was a fatigue induced auditory hallucination. I couldn't cope with any more drama.

"Open up now, man. It's the police," said the voice.

I smiled with relief and unchained the security latch, then swung the door open. Chris stood before me, his hand raised in an attitude of solidarity with Black Power, poised for more knocking.

"Oh! It's you!" he squealed.

"What are you doing here, Chris?" I asked.

He looked at me for a moment. "I heard about what happened with you and Callum," he said. "And I saw a light on and I thought you were, like, an unwanted visitor. So I came to investigate."

"But...?"

"I was just passing by, man," Chris shrugged, his broken boxer's grin widening. "Scared you, d..ln't I? You thought I was the police."

"Yes," I lied, and ushered him inside.

"Yeah." Chris paused. "But hey, you're not supposed to be here either. Why aren't you up at your dad's castle?" He stopped abruptly and looked at me, then looked down at his hands. There was an awkwardness between us. "So... Is your dad... I mean..."

"He's the same as before. Dying slowly."

Chris let out a staccato spray of embarrassed laughter. "Jesus, Pip. Your dad's kickin' it. You just split with your boyfriend. I'm going to have to come around more often! Don't you have any *good* news?"

"Yes, as a matter of fact I do!" I cried, which startled Chris. "I'm going to be in *Rat Trap*."

"That new police series? I heard about that."

"Detective Spencer," I told him, pointing towards my own chest.

"No shit! That's brilliant, man." Chris clapped me on the

shoulder with his enormous hand, and looked at me sideways for a while. "Will you be, like, rich?" he said.

"I don't know. No, not rich exactly. But it's a good whack."

"You couldn't lend me some dosh, could you?"

I had to admire Chris's ability to get straight to the point, and his eye for a soft touch. It was the child in him.

"Get out of town," I told him affectionately.

Chris gave me another sideways look. "So, does this call for a celebratory drink, or what?"

"It most certainly does," I told him. "But not tonight. I've got to get up early for a wardrobe call tomorrow. That's why I'm here."

"Okay. Right. I'll definitely take you up on that. And remember: You're paying."

"Naturally," I replied. "Now, leave me alone. I've got to get to bed."

"Oh god, he's getting starry already," Chris pouted, then grinned. "Okay, I'm history. I'll catch you later."

The wardrobe call was swift and tedious, and it turned out that I could have given them all the required information over the phone, which I found annoying. Even so, it wasn't until ten thirty that I was ready to leave. Once again I had to rush. Hélène needed to leave by twelve.

As I wound through the Norfolk countryside, which grew flatter and ever more depressing the further northeast I drove, my thoughts turned back to Harry and his illness. How ill was he? How long would he survive, staggering along in this half-life he presently inhabited? I knew that, however long it was, I would have to be there for him. And in that moment the cold realisation hit me: there might be an impossible clash with *Rat Trap*. It felt like a knife piercing my solar plexus.

168

But at the same time, another part of me knew that I could not turn the job down. It was the best chance I'd ever been offered, and I would be a fool pass it up. I had already done my duty, surely? Far more than that, in fact. When the time came, Hélène would have to take over from me. It was as simple as that. It wouldn't be for long. But I knew that she couldn't do it. She was about to begin a major case and was not available as an understudy. The only other option was to turn him over to the medics. That was the strong choice. The choice which proved once and for all that I was my own man, that the bond between Harry and me – if bond there was at all – was as brittle as a winter twig. But I knew I couldn't do that. I felt guilty enough about Harry's fall. I'd feel even worse if I walked away now and consigned him to his own personal terror – doctors. As I neared home and wound down the drive to Ravencrag Yard, I knew I would not do that to him.

And then, as I parked and stepped out of the car, another possibility presented itself in my mind. Harry was very ill now. There was a chance that he might die before any decision had to be made... As soon as the thought occurred to me I felt guilty, and I pushed it away.

On entering the house, I was immediately greeted by Hélène. She looked tired, her countenance pinched and grey. Clearly, she had not slept.

"Harry's been asking for you," she said.

"Is he all right?" I said, concerned.

"Oh yes. But I can't do anything right, according to him. He wants you."

I stared at her, astonished. "He's speaking?" He'd hardly been able to breathe when I left him.

"Yes. He's much better today. He's still very weak, but he can definitely talk. Or rather, complain."

I shook my head. He was crawling back from the precipice again.

"Did the costume fitting go well?" she asked as we walked down the hall to where Harry lay.

"Yes." I delivered a wan smile, like thin spring sunshine.

My sister stooped down and hugged me. "Well done, little brother. Mum would have been so pleased." Then she released me from her arms. "Now come and sort Harry out. He's driving me demented. I don't know how you can stand it."

I poked my head round the sitting room door and looked at my tiny father, propped up against a mountain of pillows. The bedclothes hardly seemed to acknowledge his presence.

"Hello," I said. And then the phone rang. "I'll just answer that," I told him. "I'll be down in a minute."

Harry executed a dismissive nod of his head, as if I was a servant, and I rolled my eyes at Hélène. Then I trotted back down the corridor to the phone.

"Hello Pip," said the familiar voice of my agent. His tone was buoyant, a mood I couldn't match. "How's things?"

"Okay. The wardrobe call was fine."

"Good." My agent paused. "Anyway, I'm ringing with some more details. Your first script's in the post, and you're also wanted for some dumb exterior location shots."

"Uh-huh. When?"

"That's the tricky part. You're officially on stand-by as of now. Apparently they're waiting for a particular weather condition to coincide with a particular event, in Woolwich."

"Ah," I deadpanned.

"It's good news," my agent chirruped. "It means you get paid as of now, just to sit at home and wait."

"I suppose so."

"So you can expect a call from a Maggie Taylor at some stage. She's the Second Assistant. And don't worry, Pip," my agent added, pausing to clear his throat, "they are aware of your circumstances."

I smiled a private smile, thinking that they didn't know the half of it. "Okay. Thanks," I said, and rang off.

I returned to the sitting room, dragging my hand along the dark, uneven surface of the wall as I went, as I had done as a child. When I reached the door I looked down at my fingertips, and saw that they were covered in a thin film of dust. As I rubbed the dust away, I heard raised voices, and Harry mentioning my name. I waited outside and listened.

"Where has he gone now?" Harry carped, his thin voice a childish whine. "First he leaves without telling me, then he comes back and ignores me."

"He's not ignoring you. He came in to say hello a moment ago. He'll be back in a minute."

"He doesn't care, that boy. Always did do exactly as he pleased. It shouldn't surprise me now."

Hélène emitted a strangled noise. "How can you say that?" she said. "He's been looking after you for weeks."

"Where is he now, then?"

"I'll tell you precisely where he is," Hélène said, her big voice sounding impossibly strong after my father's thin warble. "He's in the hall, talking to his agent."

"Typical."

"For your information, we do actually have lives independent of you," Hélène shouted. Her choler had risen. She was at full steam, the way she was when blasting someone with a shaky defence. "Not that you'd ever ask!"

There was a long pause, and I took this opportunity to enter the room. Harry and Hélène both looked at me as I came in.

"You're feeling better, I see," I told my father, but he would not meet my eye and turned away.

After a difficult, frozen moment the mood changed. Something melted, and Hélène's expression became intense, yet soft. She looked at Harry with her lips pressed together and the pink end of her tongue protruding, which lent her a sudden, uncanny resemblance to Kate. It was the expression our mother had always worn when she was painting. And of course Hélène was painting now. She was painting Harry's sick face on to the canvas of her mind. She knew this was the last time she'd see him alive.

"What?" said Harry, as if we had said something.

Hélène gave a taut smile, and sat down on the bed. "I have to leave now, dad. I've got a big case on, and the hearing starts today."

"Anything good?" he asked her.

She shrugged. "The charge is murder."

I was impressed. "Prosecuting or defending?" I said.

"Defending." She leant forward and kissed Harry on the forehead, choosing the exact spot where I had planted my injudicious kiss, weeks before, then got up and smoothed out her clothes. "I can't think of anything I want to do less, at the moment."

"Did he do it?" Harry enquired from the bed as Hélène's big hand turned the brass door knob.

"Oh yes," my sister told him. "But it's a she, not a he. There's no doubt she did it, but we are citing long-term mental cruelty as mitigation. I don't know how it will run. Some women have got off completely, with that plea. If her story is true, she deserves to."

"I'll see you to the door," I said, and followed my sister out of the room as she and Harry tossed over-casual goodbyes to one another.

When the moment came for us to part, we stood on the porch step like a pair of mismatched bookends. We didn't say anything for a long time, just hugged one another. Being the smaller and weaker, I was the first to give up, and stepped away.

"I won't be coming back, Pip, at the end," she told me.

"I know. I guessed that." I gave her an encouraging smile. "It's a kind of role reversal this time around."

Hélène's eyes misted with tears. "I'm sorry, Pip. I feel so guilty."

This surprised me. Hélène had as little connection with Harry as I did. "Why?" I said.

"I've acted appallingly over this. Looking after Harry, I mean. I didn't realise he could be so... difficult. You shouldn't have had to do it all on your own. You should have had help."

I shrugged. "Don't be stupid. Now, how can I get in touch with you, if I need to, during this trial?"

"You can always reach me on my mobile," she said. "Ring me if there's any news, won't you?"

"Yes," I assured her. "Of course I will." I gave her a lightning peck on the cheek. "Good luck with the case."

"Thanks." She sighed again. "God, do I look as bad as I feel?"

"How bad do you feel?"

Finally, Hélène laughed. I waved her away. "Go and defend your murderess," I told her.

"See you, little brother," she said, and then she was gone.

For some time I stood motionless on the doorstep, like an idiot, listening to the quiet rush of her tyres on the driveway as she wound away towards the main road. The silence that followed seemed more profound, more lonely, than any I had previously encountered.

I didn't want to go back into the house. I wanted to run blindly though the paddocks and bury myself in End Wood; I wanted to lean against a tree, tilt my head upward, and howl to the sky for my mother; and I wanted it all to end. But the end was not in sight. I was still here at Ravencrag, alone with my estranged, dying father. It was with reluctance that I went back inside to join him.

For his part, the life seemed to flow out of Harry as the day wore on. His lungs seemed to lose power again, and he had to concentrate on the slow drawing in and release of each breath. Once again, talk became a luxury. He even had to retreat behind his oxygen mask later on, but I didn't take this as a bad sign. He had yo-yoed to and from the brink so many times that I had suspended my judgement. He was as likely to die now as he was to wake up and suggest a short walk. Far into the night, I fell asleep in my chair with the heat from the Norwegian stove on my cheeks. The sound of Harry's breathing, which underscored my every thought, was like feeble waves on a distant beach. Towards dawn, I fitted a new vial of medication into Harry's pump, and realised that I had no idea what drug it was. Morphine? Something for the PCP? I decided, in the end, that it didn't matter.

In the morning, Harry seemed stable – neither better nor worse. I, on the other hand, had a stiff neck and a sore back from sleeping in the chair again, and hobbled about with a geriatric shuffle. The weather was gloomy and damp, the sky bruised by a low ceiling of blue-black cloud, and a strong wind was getting up. I felt hemmed in, caged from all sides.

At ten-o-clock, I ordered two more cylinders of oxygen, as Harry's current one was running low. There were no runners available from the hospital, so I arranged to have them collected by taxi. The practice seemed bizarre, and startled the taxi company I phoned. It took some moments to convince them that it was not a hoax call. When the cylinders arrived, I staggered down to the sitting room with them, one by one, and managed to gouge a chunk out of the door frame as I did so.

"Reinforcements," I told Harry, who looked at me with questioning eyes as I came in with the second.

"Thank you," he mouthed through his mask.

The remark brought me up short. It was the first time he'd thanked me for anything since I'd arrived here. For some reason it made me uncomfortable.

As the morning progressed, a thick, unnatural silence came between us, redolent with the events of the past few days, which served only to heighten the clamour of the elements outside. I could hear the angry wind tearing through the cherry trees in the garden, and the rattle of occasional sudden bursts of rain on the window. It felt like the end of something. Restless, I stared out of the window at the low sky then shuffled back to my armchair feeling more depressed than I'd ever been. Outside, a storm was ripening, but inside, all was still. Too still. A great, suffocating blanket had been laid over the world, lowering my horizon until it included only myself and Harry. Nothing else seemed real, and I couldn't remember ever having had any other life.

I stood beside Harry's bed for a while and watched him breathing with furious effort, his feeble, bubbling lungs ever greedier for air, and wondered how much more I could take. I decided that he looked worse than he had when I'd gone to phone for the oxygen, and suddenly I was afraid to leave him alone. What if he needed me when I was out of the room? I decided to bring the phone into the sitting room, and fetch some sandwiches, then I wouldn't have to go out at all.

This proved wise, because at eleven, Harry's oxygen tank ran out. His eyes grew wide with panic as he discovered that ordinary air, air good enough for my lungs, was not sufficient to sustain him. As fast as I could, I began to change over to a new tank, but my hands were shaking and slowed me down. Half way through the process the phone began to ring, on and on, an insistent backdrop to my fumbling efforts to let my father breathe, which lent extra urgency to the moment and made me fumble still more. As I worked, Harry's face began to turn pale blue, his thin lips almost translucent, and then at last I had the valve switched on and pure oxygen rushed into his lungs and he began to respond.

Sweating and breathless, I answered the phone at last. It seemed to have been ringing forever.

"Hello. May I speak to Pip Winter, please?"

"Speaking. Who is this?"

"I'm Maggie Taylor from *Rat Trap*. I'm ringing about your call."

"Yes?"

"We'd like you to come in later today, please."

I groaned audibly. Why did everything happen at such short notice? It was ridiculous.

"I know you're not in London," Maggie Taylor continued, "but could you make it to the Woolwich ferry for two?"

"I'm afraid not," I replied in a strangled voice. "It's not possible."

"You do know you're on call?"

"Yes. Of course. But I can't leave my father now. He's very ill. Can't you film these exterior shots some other time?"

"Unfortunately, no. We have to film them today, or not at all. It's the only time the location will be free during this weather. It's vital to the whole series. It's being inter-cut into each episode."

"Sorry. I can't do it," I told her in a leaden voice. I felt like an assassin. The victim was my career.

"But you're under contract. You must!" She sounded harassed and desperate, but I couldn't help that.

"I said I *can't*," I yelled, then slammed the phone down. And for an instant I had an inkling of the despair that Callum must have felt as I pushed him out of the door for the last time.

I sighed, and squeezed my eyes tight shut for a moment. That was it, I thought, I no longer had a job. When I opened them again and turned round, Harry was staring up at me with an odd expression on his face.

Towards the end of the afternoon, during which we sat watching children's tv together, not speaking, Harry beckoned me over. I sat down on the side of his bed. He looked at me with his watery Walt Disney eyes and slowly reached for my face with his hand. He pressed his chilly palm to my cheek with the rapt expression of one seeing a vision, and I froze inside. It was the first time – at least, the first I could remember – that Harry had ever touched me lovingly. Had he decided that in turning down *Rat Trap*, I had proved that I loved him? I tried to smile, and tucked his hand back beneath the covers.

Feeling bereft, I sat by the stove for the remainder of the afternoon, and thought about a folk tale I'd been told at school called *The Rolling Rice*. In the story there was a village in China, and every year on a certain date these enormous grains of rice would roll down from the mountains for the people to eat – one giant grain for each family, which would last a whole year. Each spring, the people had to build a special hut for the rice to roll into. One year, a man got greedy and wanted two grains of giant rice, but he didn't have time to complete two huts, and the rice rolled down from the mountains before the second one was finished. 'Stop. Go back. My hut isn't finished,' he said, and all the rice rolled out of the village again, back up into the mountains, never to return, and the village starved. And that was how I felt now. I thought I would never be offered another job ever again, because I had turned this one down.

Heavy, sad, and morose, I prodded at the glowing, scintillating logs in the stove with the poker, occasionally taking another from the neat stack on the hearth and throwing it in. I felt desolate for more reasons than I could name. Early darkness pressed around the house like a weight, and I allowed my face to get red and hot as I leant forward with my elbows on my knees, staring fixedly into the fire until my eyes began to smart.

Harry developed a wheezing rattle in his throat mid evening, which sounded like a rake over pebbles. The tendons in his neck stood out as he struggled for breath, and I sat beside him on the bed, staring down into his clouded eyes. He was clearly frightened, and this puzzled me. He believed in God and Heaven. He had been saved. Surely his ticket to the afterlife was booked? Why, then, did he have such fear? But then I realised: he had been promised a cure, and it had not been forthcoming. He knew he'd backed the wrong horse.

I reached down for his hand, which lay beneath the covers, and applied the gentlest of pressures to it. "It's okay," I said.

Harry looked up at me with the face of a broken man and mouthed something, but I couldn't decipher his words – the movement of his lips was too erratic. He frowned, and tried again. I still couldn't work it out.

"I don't understand what you're saying," I told him.

Harry drew his hands from under the covers and tried to remove the mask, but I restrained him, gently. I didn't think it was a good idea. I knew he would not be able to breathe. But he shook his head at me. I let my hands fall and watched as he slipped the mask off his face. For a few seconds he opened and closed his mouth like a fish, then he gasped out his message.

"The... fall... down... stairs."

I was amazed at his capacity for denial, but I understood. I looked at him and slipped the mask back over his mouth. We both knew neither of us really believed what he had said.

At half past nine the phone rang, shattering the unnatural silence which had settled over us. I was in no mood to talk to anybody and slouched to the phone like an old man.

"Pip, it's Jim Johnson."

My whole body tensed, and at the same time a wave of profound fatigue coursed through me. This was the conversation that I could live without, the ritual roasting for turning down a perfect job. I felt certain that he was calling to say that he no longer wanted to represent me, and I wasn't sure if I could even be bothered to explain myself.

"Hello, Jim," I managed, my voice rough with tiredness.

"Look, I'm sorry to call you late like this," my agent said, "but I've just been talking to Maggie Taylor..."

"From *Rat Trap*?"

"Yes. She wasn't at all pleased with your stunt, you know. She was on at me for half an hour this morning." My agent paused. "But that's not why I'm ringing."

"Oh?"

"No. She phoned just now to tell me that it rained."

I didn't understand. "What for?"

My agent softened his tone in response to my mood. "It rained – in Woolwich – all afternoon," he said, "so your presence was not required after all."

My mind was sluggish, and I wasn't certain if I had heard him correctly.

"Oh," I said.

My agent gave a friendly, avuncular laugh. "Isn't that good news?"

"Yes," I said. It was the only response I could muster.

It seemed that I was was still in with a chance of keeping the part, but the news did not penetrate the cocoon of despondency which had encased me. I knew that there would be a time, in the future, when I would be excited by it, but not now. I was too numb. Too much was going on. All I could do was to put it to one side, to be dealt with later.

"Okay, then. We'll talk again soon," my agent said, and rang off.

At once, the night thickened around Ravencrag, strengthening its grip on Harry and me, and I felt remote, removed from the world. I didn't try to read, it was impossible. Instead, I watched the progress of the carved hands of the Swiss cuckoo clock as they wound round and round its baroque face, and with each sweep of the minute hand, the tourniquet of grim anticipation which had been applied to my heart grew tighter. I could sense, as well as see, that Harry was losing his fight for breath, but I did not call Dr Daniels out. There was nothing he could do, and Harry did not appear to be in discomfort. It was better this way. Harry's descent had been quick, and much more humane than the endless winding road of decline that so many others were forced to take.

Towards midnight his breathing altered again. I went over to look at him, and it was as if he were a different person. His countenance had actually changed. Gone was the tension and the fear, and his face was relaxed. He looked strangely beatific, almost holy. I sat down beside him.

He opened his eyes when he felt my weight on the bed, and smiled. Then, with papery, translucent hands, he removed the mask from his face and pushed it right up over his head, as if he had no further need for it. Immediately he convulsed. His chest seemed to implode, as if he were in a vacuum, and his face adopted a series of alarming colours in rapid succession, like a chameleon. But he was smiling, and his eyes were clear.

Suddenly he sat up, with a fluidity and power that startled me, and stretched out his arms – a child demanding a hug. In an automatic response I opened my own arms, and my bony father sighed against my chest. The room was silent. I sat on the bed with Harry in my arms – hugging him the way I had always wanted him to hug me, the way he never had – and felt the last whisper of breath leave his body. It brushed past me like a cobweb, and then he was gone.

I didn't know what I had expected of the final moment, but it wasn't this. There was no pain, no sense of loss, no relief, no guilt even. There was only absence of feeling. I didn't move for some time, and kept very still, frozen in this attitude of Madonna and child. And as I sat in the dim room cradling my dead parent I was reminded, abstrusely, of that song in *A Chorus Line*, 'Nothing.' That was it. I felt nothing, which was infinitely worse that anything I could have imagined.

I phoned Hélène, and told her that our father had died. Like me, she seemed curiously detached.

"I'll make all the relevant calls," she offered. "You've done enough."

"Thanks," I said. "I'd appreciate that."

"Are you all right up there?"

"Yes," I said. "I think so. But it's odd. I feel a tremendous sense of, I don't know, anti-climax."

"Yes," she told me. "It's because you've been waiting for it to happen for too long."

"Probably."

I put the phone down and cradled it in my lap as I stared at the wall. But I found I couldn't stay in the room with my father, and wandered aimlessly round the house, turning on all the lights. Ravencrag felt so *empty* that I had to fill it with something. It wasn't until I snapped on the last bedroom light that it occurred to me that Harry had done the same thing the night Kate had died. Harry, too, had felt the weight of emptiness pressing in on him, and had needed to escape its oppression. He had wanted to blaze out the loss of his wife of thirty years. And in that moment I realised that I had, perhaps, been too swift a judge of him. How could I know how he bore his pain?